The Family Secret
Paperback Copyright © 2021 Lorhainne Ekelund
Editor: Talia Leduc

ISBN-13: 9781989698327

Give feedback on the book at:
lorhainneeckhart@hotmail.com

Twitter: @LEckhart
Facebook: AuthorLorhainneEckhart

Printed in the U.S.A

THE FAMILY SECRET

The O'Connells

LORHAINNE ECKHART

About the O'Connells

The O'Connells of Livingston, Montana, are not your typical family. Follow them on their journey to the dark and dangerous side of love in a series of romantic thrillers you won't want to miss. Raised by a single mother after their father's mysterious disappearance eighteen years ago, the six grown siblings live in a small town with all kinds of hidden secrets, lies, and deception. Much like the contemporary family romance series focusing on the Friessens, this romantic suspense series follows the lives of the O'Connell family as each of the siblings searches for love.

The O'Connells

The Neighbor
The Third Call
The Secret Husband
The Quiet Day
The Commitment, An O'Connell Novella
The Missing Father
The Hometown Hero

Justice
The Family Secret
The Fallen O'Connell
The Return of the O'Connells
And The She Was Gone
The Stalker
The O'Connell Family Christmas
The Girl Next Door
Broken Promises
The Gatekeeper

The Family Secret

Raymond O'Connell was the love of Iris's life—from the day she met him, to the day a year later when she married him, to the tragic night before she never saw him again.

Some would say they had the perfect all-American life. Now, eighteen years later, questions arise about the night her husband disappeared, leaving a bloody knife and a letter addressed to her, in which he said goodbye and told her not to look for him, with not even a second thought for her and their six children.

The scandal when Raymond left rocked the community, fueling widespread rumors, from him running away with his mistress to him being dead. But through it all, Iris kept her head down, keeping the secret of what really happened. Although her children often wondered, and her eldest thought he was protecting her from something heinous when she asked him to get rid of the knife, what they didn't know was that their father wasn't who they thought he was. Making sure his secret didn't come out was the only way to keep her family together.

Now, Iris can no longer keep her life with Raymond O'Connell buried, because her adult children are asking questions. The only thing she can think to do to protect herself and them is to enlist the help of a lawyer, her daughter's husband, fearing that once the truth starts to surface, it could change everything about their lives.

The secret of their father, which Iris has hidden for so long now, has the potential to destroy everything the O'Connells have built for themselves, and once the truth of who Raymond O'Connell really was comes out, it will put a target on all of them, and their lives in peaceful Livingston, Montana, will never be the same.

Chapter One

At one time, if anyone had tried to tell Iris she would end up with the stable life she had now, she'd have told them they were crazy. For so many years, she'd kept her head down, putting everything on hold for her children and pushing away that hurt, that ache, that pain that had shredded her heart, having to climb out of the dark pit that wanted to drag her down.

Now, as she pulled in a breath, she had to remind herself that she no longer felt that guttural ache that had stolen her peace of mind and distracted her from all those small things that should've put a smile on her face in her children's early years. She'd forgotten exactly when it had happened, when that wretched, visceral ache, which she'd screamed into a pillow to ease, had just left.

Her six children, whom she couldn't imagine a life without, were all grown now, and she still centered everything around them. Her life was theirs. At the same time, there were days she wondered whether she had permanently scarred them, whether she could've done better.

She took in the concrete buildings, the bustling streets,

the restaurants and bars and stores, and the scent of the autumn day on the breeze. These people made Livingston her home. It was a part of who she was, though there were times she had to tell herself she wasn't a fraud.

The light of day seemed so different from the shadows of night. The darkness still called to her when she was alone, looking out into the yard. She wondered what was hiding there, what was waiting to tear down the façade she'd built and take away everything that put a smile on her face, all the reasons she could now hold her head high. It was just a feeling she couldn't shake, one that had suddenly reemerged the moment her children learned of the night she wished she could forget.

She lifted her hand in a wave at a couple she knew, then another neighbor, people she knew well had gossiped behind her back at one time after she went from being a married woman to a single mother, struggling alone with six kids. It had cut her to the quick. Yes, Raymond O'Connell had been there one day and gone the next, and the rumors about why had left her feeling more alone than anything.

Of course it still smarted, if she really thought about it now. How did one go about shaking off all those hurtful rumors? People had trashed her character, saying she wasn't good enough, that she must've done something to deserve such a fate, that she was screwing up big-time when it came to her kids, all because the O'Connells no longer fit the all-American mold of how a family was supposed to be.

She clutched her bargain-bin purse, wearing a plain white T-shirt and loose red cardigan over slimming blue jeans. She didn't have to look in a mirror to know that while she was just Mom around her grown children, any man out there would've given her a second look. It was just who she was. Even though time hadn't been her friend, her lack of money while the kids were young had kept her from eating her way into a pity party. She was grateful for that, at least, considering being slim and attractive had been the furthest thing from her mind for too many years.

She took in the nightclub in front of her, where staff were serving the lunch crowd, then turned to the glass industrial door with the words "Karen O'Connell & Jack Curtis, Lawyers" etched in black. An office over a nightclub. She couldn't help the smile that tugged at her lips.

She was so proud of her daughter Karen, a lawyer, and Karen's husband, Jack, who had a charm and charisma about him that reminded her so much of her own husband. Maybe that was why she watched him from a distance, wondering when he'd turn into someone else. There was something about him that told her he was holding on to the kind of secrets he would never share with another person. How did she know? It was just one of those feelings she got about people she spent time with.

She knew there was so much more to his life and his secrets than she would ever know, but she also knew he'd do anything for her daughter.

Iris forced herself to touch the steel handle and pull open the door, feeling it scrape against the metal lip on the ground. She started up the steps, her shoes squeaking to announce her arrival. Her palms sweated, and her heart kicked up with each step. She made herself pull in a breath.

She could hear talking, a man's voice—Jack, she thought—as she stepped up on the landing, her hand on the rail, taking in the narrow hall and the open office door. The walls were dingy, nicked, and needed a fresh coat of paint.

She stepped into the reception area, seeing the door to

Karen's office closed. Jack was sitting at the receptionist's desk, a position they still hadn't filled. He lifted his hand in a wave to her, the phone to his ear, his blue eyes mysterious and his dark hair neatly groomed. He already had a five o'clock shadow, and it was barely noon. He hung up the phone and stood.

"Iris, I didn't know you were coming by," he said, gesturing toward her and walking around the desk. "Karen is actually in court right now."

She shook her head, taking in his blue striped dress shirt and dark pants. He was attractive, and she wondered, looking at him now, what it was about him that gave her that sense of familiarity, reminding her of a man she'd once thought of dozens of times a day—a man who, thankfully, had now become just a passing thought.

"That's fine," Iris said. "I actually stopped by to see you. Do you have a minute?"

She wasn't sure what he was thinking. He hesitated, and a soft smile touched his lips as he leaned against the desk and crossed his arms, giving her everything with just a look. She glanced over her shoulder to the open door and then back to him.

"You know what?" he said. "Let's go talk in the office. Seems my wife and I can't decide on a new place. She likes this dump, and we end up having to share an office, or one of us works out in reception…" He opened the office door and walked in, then stepped aside so he could close it behind her.

He had evidently picked up on her unease and her need for privacy, even though she didn't have a clue what she was going to say. He gestured to the chairs in front of the desk, and she squeezed her purse over her shoulder.

"Please, Iris, have a seat," he said. "So you wanted to talk to me?"

She walked over to the chair and sat down, and she expected him to sit behind the desk across from her, but instead he sat beside her. Something in his blue eyes was so intense. He didn't look away, didn't pull away. He seemed amused, curious, but she wondered how curious he'd be when he learned the truth of what she'd done and who she really was.

There it was, silence, because she'd missed her cue to speak.

She slid her purse strap off her shoulder and took her time setting it on the floor. When she looked up, he was still waiting patiently.

"Is everything all right, Iris?" he said, then glanced to the door and back to her. He leaned forward, his forearms resting on his knees, and she took in the scar along the side of his face, tiny, just barely there. He started to laugh and rubbed the back of his head. "Are you upset with me or something?"

She gestured toward him. "No, no, nothing like that. I just need a second to find the words or rip the bandage off, so to speak. You know, Karen doesn't know I've come here, and neither do my other children…" She hesitated.

Jack glanced to the door again and sat up straighter, an odd smile touching his lips. "Okay. You do know that whatever you say to me, I won't share it. It stays between us."

She reached for her purse and unzipped it, then opened up her wallet, seeing the bills inside. She pulled out a dollar bill and rested it on the desk, one hand pressed over it as she clutched her wallet in the other.

He inhaled and stared at her hand. Evidently, he had figured out this was something more than a friendly visit.

"I want to hire you as my lawyer, Jack," she said, then pushed the bill closer to him.

His expression had suddenly turned serious as he

dragged his gaze over to her. His blue eyes were so different from the O'Connell blue. He hesitated, and all she did was lower her gaze to the money on the desk beside him, forcing a swallow past the lump in her throat and fighting the instinctual tremble in her hand.

"Is it true that as my lawyer, you can't share anything?" she said, though she knew it was, considering she'd listened to everything Karen had shared with her during her studies to become a lawyer—every law, all the rights, everything that could be used against someone.

Jack pulled in a breath, hesitating only a second before he settled his hand over the bill and held it up. "Okay, so this is a retainer?" He didn't laugh. He could obviously see that she had no intention of saying a word until he said what she needed to hear.

"Yes, consider me your lawyer," he said, then shoved the dollar bill in his pocket. He stood up and walked around the desk, changing from her daughter's husband to a businessman. Maybe he needed to have something between them to ensure a level of professionality.

She did, too, but more for courage, because she couldn't remember feeling the kind of fear she was feeling right now. She wondered whether he could hear her relief as she breathed out.

"So you're looking for a will or something done up?" he said. The way he asked, it sounded as if he couldn't imagine anything else. He actually reached for a legal pad in one of Karen's drawers and rummaged for a pen as Iris silently wished it were that simple.

"I married a man and had six of his children only to learn he wasn't the man I thought he was," she said. "The night he left, I did something."

Jack leaned on the desk, ready to write, and froze, pen in hand. He slowly dragged his gaze up and over to her, and she had to force herself to continue before the fear that was threatening to choke her took over and shut down her voice. Her throat was thick, and she cleared it.

"I'm afraid that one day very soon, there will be a knock on my door, a reckoning for what I did and what I know. In fact, I can already feel it, something coming, whispering that my time is up."

She'd expected shock, maybe outrage, not the stillness that was staring back at her. He opened his mouth to say something, but instead he simply stood up, walked over to the door, and locked it.

When he turned, she could see he needed a minute to get his head around the bomb she'd just dropped. He started back to the desk, digging into each step, but instead of sitting, he rested his hands on the back of the chair right beside her and leaned down. His gaze was imploring, intense, and she knew she had all his attention.

"Okay, I think you'd better start at the beginning," he said, "and don't leave anything out."

Chapter Two

Jack needed a second.

He stared at Iris, whose face was so much like his wife's. Her chest rose as she waited for him to say something, as if waiting for the other shoe to drop. The blue of her eyes resembled his wife's in some ways, but where Karen's cheeks were plump, Iris had a narrow face and nose, and her lips were not quite as full.

He realized that what she'd just said concerned something he'd always seen as a big black circle of mystery about his wife's father, just something none of the O'Connells spoke of.

Jack stood up and dragged his hand over his face, hearing the scrape of whiskers. Iris pressed her lips together, and he found himself looking to the door and hesitating, wondering when Karen would be done with her motion at the courthouse and back. It could be hours or minutes.

"I'm not sure where to start," Iris finally said.

It wasn't as if Jack had trouble getting clients to talk, but everyone was different, and this was Iris O'Connell, his wife's mother, his family. "Well, let's start with the fact that you're here to see me. I need to ask, does Karen know about whatever this is?"

She hesitated and glanced away. "Not everything, only the part that Owen knew. My son came downstairs just as I had wrapped up the knife in some cloth. The office was a mess, broken things, paper everywhere, and there was blood. I asked Owen to get rid of the knife. I never really considered what he thought, because he never said anything. But apparently, he buried it in the woods. This just came out now. Someone saw him do it, that lady who was part of the recent high school trouble. I know Owen and Marcus have taken care of it now. They got the knife back. That woman had something on us, something that would prompt questions I don't want to answer. I didn't realize what Owen thought I had done until he and Marcus came to me. Suzanne was there, and Luke was home, too. They don't know that I know this, but they shared it with Ryan and Karen even though I asked them not to… But they don't know everything." Her knuckles were white from gripping her purse.

"How is it possible that I believed someone I was so close and intimate with, then learned that everything was a lie? I told Owen that I needed his help to keep us together. Like, what the fuck is wrong with me? Owen was just a kid, a teenager. He went from just a typical sixteen-year-old to a father figure overnight, having to watch over his siblings. I knew it, but I was drowning in everything, trying to figure out how to put one foot in front of the other." She sighed.

He realized he'd never had this kind of trouble before with a client, worrying about whether they had done the worst thing imaginable. Often, they had, but in this case, he wasn't sure he wanted to know. What the hell was he going to tell Karen?

Nothing.

"So there was a knife and blood and a crime scene, and you basically…"

"Cleaned up," she said. "I think that's what you're getting at. Yes, Jack, I cleaned up a crime scene. I cleaned up the office, I destroyed evidence, I dragged my impressionable teenage son into something unknowingly because he walked into the middle of everything as I was trying to wrap my head around it. You know what? That night has been with me for so long, yet there I was, all these years later, thinking it had finally stopped haunting me. I had spent night after night trying to make sense of what happened."

She killed him, he thought. It was his first thought, yet he couldn't ask. "Go on," he said. "Tell me everything, Iris, so I can figure out how to help."

She merely nodded. He could see how shallow her breathing was. This wasn't the Iris O'Connell he was used to, who was always smiling and laughing with her kids. "Raymond had been acting strangely for some time, and I suspected he was involved in something, but I kept telling myself it was nothing. Have you ever known someone so well and then realized one day that you didn't know anything about them? I did."

She didn't let him answer. He could see how she was struggling to find the words. "I just told myself I likely didn't want to know, or it was nothing. Men I'd never seen before had started showing up late, when the kids were in bed, when I was getting ready to turn in for the night and expecting Raymond to follow. He'd started keeping to his office downstairs. When I came home with the kids to make dinner, there were times I found him there instead of at work. He was good with his hands, could fix anything. But he became dismissive, secretive, and I could feel him pushing me away. Then that night happened…"

That was all she said. Then she coughed.

"Let me get you some water," Jack said, striding over to the small bar fridge. He opened it and reached for one of the bottles his wife kept stocked for him, then closed the fridge and took a second before turning around. Held out the water to her.

"Thank you." She unscrewed the cap and took a swallow.

Jack took in the legal pad waiting on the desk for him to write something. His wife's mother was confessing to something she'd done, and right now, he was positive this knowledge would be just something else that could come between him and his wife.

"So let's go back to that night," he said. "You said there were men there. Who were these men?"

She pulled in a breath and glanced down. "You know, Jack, I don't know who they were. I'd never seen them before. I'd only heard voices and gone down once, and I saw a man, balding, sitting with my husband. The other standing. I'd never seen him before. But have you ever met someone and realized there was something about them, something that made you swear you'd never forget their face? Well, there was something about them that bothered me.

"That was the first time Raymond ever dismissed me— you know, telling me to go to bed, that he had business that didn't concern me. I wanted to stand my ground and tell him where to go, but the way he looked at me and the amusement on the stranger's face… I left. Of course, I waited for him, but I eventually fell asleep. I'm not even sure he came to bed. I was furious, and you know what I did? I ate that anger. I didn't speak. Then I realized after days that he wasn't going to apologize. That was the first time that it seemed as if he'd suddenly changed into a different person. He was no longer the tall, dashing, dark-haired, blue-eyed devil who'd arrived in town one day and swept me off my feet, a man who'd turned my life, our life, into a dream. It had turned into a nightmare."

He was pacing now, his arms across his chest. "I'm not understanding what happened. You need to tell me what you did. Did you hurt him?"

She made a face and started to say something, but she pulled in a breath, and her jaw slackened. She glanced over to the window and shook her head before looking back to him. "There was a letter on his desk, in his handwriting. All it said was 'Goodbye. Don't look for me. I'm sorry.' The problem is, Jack, I had woken up on the floor of his office and seen the mess and the blood, and I didn't remember what had happened or how I'd got there. All I knew was that I was suddenly standing in the middle of something gruesome, bloody, and I had no idea where my husband was…"

He was positive there was more. He stared at her as she lowered her head, looking down at her hands, flexing them and holding her ringless fingers out in front of her as if they held all the answers.

"Are you telling me you woke up in a crime scene, and there was blood, a knife, and a messy room, and you don't know how you got there? You remember nothing? Were you knocked out? You didn't call the police?"

She shook her head, and for a minute, he had to remind himself this was Karen's mother, because if it had been anyone else, he'd have told them he didn't believe them.

"I don't understand why you didn't call the police, the sheriff," he said. "That makes absolutely no sense, Iris."

"You don't get it, Jack?" she said.

He just stared at her, because none of this made any sense. "No. Fill me in, Iris, because from where I'm sitting, you haven't given me one reason yet why you couldn't have called the police. Why didn't you report him missing? People had to wonder where he was. He had a job, right?"

All Iris did was lift her blue eyes to him, and this time her expression was filled with a confidence he wasn't entirely comfortable with. "Reporting him missing wasn't an option," she said, "because when I woke up, the knife was in my hand."

Chapter Three

When Ryan O'Connell stepped inside his house, he froze. The TV was displaying some videogame he'd never seen before, and Alison was on the sofa with a lanky teenage boy who had short dark hair and long legs, wearing blue jeans and a gray T-shirt. They were sitting side by side, controllers in hand, playing some guns-blasting game, which he had no idea his daughter had any interest in.

No, scratch that. He knew she hated everything about videogames.

He paused for a second, feeling dusty and dirty from the trail and hearing a clatter from the kitchen just as Eva came racing through the front door behind him, followed by Charlotte, who was appearing more pregnant every day, in a T-shirt and yoga pants, her long dark hair hanging loose.

"Didn't know Alison had a boyfriend," Charlotte said. "Aren't they cute together?"

His sister-in-law's comment had him taking another look at the boy as he stood there. He should go upstairs and shower and change, but he stared at his daughter, who was sitting far too close to that boy, a young man who could've been older than her.

Charlotte called Eva into the kitchen, but Ryan still couldn't pull his gaze from Alison. She was smiling an unusual smile that he'd never seen before, and it appeared she was ignoring him. Her shirt was soft green, v-cut, and showed the curve of her breasts indecently. Like, where the hell had she gotten that shirt? Had Jenny just let her walk out of the house dressed like that?

"Didn't know you liked video games," he said, unable to stop himself, as he stepped into the living room, his hands on his hips.

Alison instantly went from smiling to looking as though she might bite his head off. As she looked up at him, he didn't miss the mascara, liner, and eye shadow that made her appear way older than her sixteen years. She said nothing, but he'd have been a fool to miss the way she gripped that controller a lot harder. She wanted him to leave, of course. Then there was the fact that she still hadn't answered him.

"I'm Alison's father," he finally said, dragging his gaze back to the boy as he stood right in front of the TV. "And you are?"

The boy stood up, and for a minute, by the way his eyes appeared bigger, he thought he was scared shitless. Good!

"My name is Brady, sir," he said. "I go to school with Alison." Then, as if he thought he should, he held out his hand.

Ryan kept his hands resting on his hips and stared at the outstretched hand for one second and then another before shaking it. The handshake was a little soft; maybe that was why Ryan squeezed harder. He looked down at

Alison, whose dark eyes, her mother's eyes, looked up at him with a ton of teenage misery. Her arms were now crossed, which did nothing to hide the fact that her breasts were barely covered by that shirt.

"So where do you live, exactly?" Ryan said. "Close by? You said you go to school with my daughter?"

"Mom…!" Alison shouted, then stood up and stomped out of the room.

Ryan made no motion to move, taking in the confusion on Brady's face as he looked over to Alison leaving and seemed to realize he was standing before a man who could make his life a living hell. Oh, Ryan hoped he believed that—and by the way he swallowed a thick lump, much like a poacher caught red handed, he did.

"Actually, not far," the boy said. "My dad and I just moved here, just up the block."

He let the boy pull his hand away. What the hell was his name again? Right, Brady. He was now sweating, and Ryan didn't pull his gaze from him, considering what else to ask a kid who appeared too much like the boy next door, a boy who could have some unhealthy ideas about his daughter. He heard a squeak of the floorboards but didn't look over, hearing footsteps coming his way.

"So are you in the same classes as my daughter?" Ryan said. "What do your parents do? What made you move here? You said something about your dad—just you and your dad?"

Brady was tall, close to his height, and seemed to shuffle in front of him. Ryan crossed his arms the way he did when questioning someone who was doing something they knew they shouldn't. Maybe he should add in another couple questions. He half expected the kid to make an excuse and head for the door. He hoped he would.

"Yeah, Alison's cool. She's in my earth science class. She makes a boring class fun."

Fun, his daughter? He wondered if his eyes bugged out.

"And yeah, it's just me and my dad. My mom died when I was a little kid…"

A hand touched his arm, and he was forced to pull his gaze from the kid, still trying to figure out the extent of Brady's interest in his daughter. He was very well aware of the kinds of things that went on in the minds of teenage boys, considering he used to be one. A seventeen- or eighteen year-old boy's hormones were the exact kind he didn't want around his daughter.

He felt the squeeze on his arm again and glanced down to his fiancée, Jenny, whose dark hair was pulled up, her cheeks plump and her lips full.

She took him in with an odd smile. "Excuse me, Ryan, can you help me in the kitchen? I need your help reaching something."

Was she kidding? "Now?" he said. "You need it right now? What is it? Just give me a minute."

But her hand slipped in his, and she was pulling him out of the living room when he hadn't even made his point yet, found out who the kid's dad was and why he'd moved there, and let Brady know exactly what his expectations were when it came to his daughter.

"No, it can't wait," Jenny said. "Come on. I need it now."

He glanced back to his daughter, whose expression was unsmiling. Alison said something to Brady, and then Ryan was pulled into the kitchen, where Charlotte was laughing, perched on a stool at the island. Eva was beside her with a small bowl of potato chips, munching.

Jenny let go of his hand and walked over to rest a

cutting board on the island along with a bag of carrots. Then she picked up the knife and started slicing one.

"So what do you need me to get down?" he said, looking around.

All Jenny did was roll her eyes and let out a sigh. Charlotte was still laughing softly. He took in Jenny's multicolored blouse, her blue jeans, and the ring he'd given her because she'd finally said yes.

"Nothing, it's just that you're intruding. So you stay here and out of the way."

"What? I'm what? What the hell?" He found himself looking over to Charlotte, who was giving him everything, a big smile on her face, laughing again. Little Eva appeared confused when Charlotte slid her hands over her ears.

"You're giving Brady the third degree, and Alison is furious. She's scared you're going to run him off," Jenny said, so matter of fact. "So you just stay in here with us. You leave her be. He's a nice boy. He just moved here with his dad, he's polite, and…"

"He's a teenage boy who has only one thing on his mind—and what the hell is she wearing, anyway? Did you see her shirt? She may as well not be wearing anything at all…"

Charlotte was still laughing as she leaned over Eva, her hands still pressed over her ears. He heard a car door outside.

The look Jenny gave him, hand on hip, was something he'd seen only a time or two. "Yes, it's rather revealing," she said, "but pick your battles. She's sixteen, Ryan, and you know what? I'd rather she wear what she's wearing now than what she used to, remember? And might I point out that she brought him home, you know, here with us, rather than sneaking around, doing God knows what? She brought him here, under this roof, where your family is coming over, everyone. They're right in the next room, playing video games, not out someplace, getting in trouble…"

"She hates video games," he started, and this time Charlotte let her hands drop because she was laughing so hard. Eva just stared up at him with a look of confusion.

"Ryan O'Connell, you know nothing about women," Jenny said. "It's not about the video games. It's about the boy. She likes him, so she's playing video games because he likes them. She invited him over because she wants to be with him. So you're going to stay in here and let Alison have her fun with a nice boy, a boy who, by the way, in case I didn't point this out, Alison wants everyone to meet. You know it's family night, and when the rest of your family shows up here and he has to talk to them, Alison and I would rather him not run screaming from the house because of an angry father who wants to kill him. She wants him to come back, and I want him to come back—here, where we live, under this roof, so she doesn't have to start sneaking around! Understand?"

"Hello…?" It was Karen.

He heard the door slap closed but didn't turn to look. He was pretty sure she was now in the living room, saying something to Alison and Brady. "Well, it sounds like Karen's in there now. Are you planning on pulling her out, too?"

Jenny opened the door of the fridge, twisted the cap off a beer, and handed it to him. "Nope, because your sister isn't going to scare him off."

Just then, Karen walked into the kitchen. "Alison has a boyfriend?" she said in a low voice.

He could see the front door open again to reveal

Suzanne, alone, and Owen and Tessa walking up to the house behind her.

"So where's Mom? Thought she'd be here," Ryan said, dragging his gaze back to the women.

"Your mom had a meeting or something," Charlotte said. "She said she couldn't take Eva today, so I took a rest day, as Marcus insisted. We had some girl time."

"Yup, me and Charlotte made a cake, chocolate," Eva said, looking up, and he couldn't help rustling her hair.

"Speaking of which, it's cooling, but Marcus can go and bring it over when he gets here," Charlotte added.

"Yum, sounds good. So what meeting?" Ryan said. Since when did his mom have meetings to go to?

Jenny just shrugged, and Charlotte gave him an odd look and shook her head as if he'd asked a stupid question.

"Who has a meeting?" Owen said, his arm across Tessa's shoulders, as the two strode into the kitchen.

Ryan was still getting used to this relaxed version of Owen. They were both in blue jeans and jean jackets. He knew his brother was spending all his time at Tessa's, and it wouldn't surprise him if he put his own house up for sale.

"Mom," Ryan told him. "Charlotte was just saying she had a meeting today, so she couldn't take Eva."

Suzanne rested a case of beer on the counter, then opened the fridge and started putting it in. The fridge was stuffed with food and the beer he'd already picked up days ago, so she left the rest on the counter in the box. "Oh, is that why Mom was at your office, Karen?" she tossed out over her shoulder.

Everyone looked at Karen, who had an odd expression. "I haven't seen Mom today," she said. "I was in court and came right from there. You're sure…?"

"Uh-huh," Suzanne said. "Saw Mom downtown as I was dropping Harold off at work. His car is in the shop.

Saw her go inside your office. Just figured she was there to see you."

Karen shrugged as her phone dinged, and she rested her purse on the counter and pulled it out, making a face. "Jack's going to be late. He's meeting with a client," she said.

Everyone said nothing for a second.

"Suzanne, why don't you call her and see if she's on her way over?" Ryan said, nodding to her, though she already had her cell phone out and was texting. Apparently, she was on it.

"Excuse me, Mr. and Mrs. O'Connell..." It was Brady, and there was Alison beside him, watching him in a way that said she thought he walked on water. "Just wanted to thank you for letting me come over and hang with Alison."

"You're not leaving, are you?" Jenny said.

Suzanne and Karen seemed to have gotten into a huddle, but whatever they were saying, he couldn't hear it. Owen gave everything to Brady and Alison, then kissed Tessa's cheek and opened the fridge to pull out two beers.

"I told Brady it was okay to stay for dinner," Alison said.

Ryan took in the boy. He was tall and a little too good looking, in his mind. He had this manner about him that seemed too charming, too charismatic.

"Yeah, please, Brady, stay for dinner. You're more than welcome," Jenny said, then angled her head toward him, her eyes imploring. Ryan knew there was an expectation in that look.

"Of course, you're welcome to stay, Brady," he finally added, wondering whether there was an edge in his voice.

"Thanks for the offer, Mr. and Mrs. O'Connell..." he started.

"Call me Jenny, Brady."

"Thank you, Jenny, and…" Maybe it was something in Ryan's expression and the way he stared down at him that made Brady's smile fade. There was no way Ryan was letting the kid use the same level of informality with him. "…Mr. O'Connell. But my dad's just called, and I need to go home. He's expecting me."

Ryan simply jutted out his chin in response to Brady's wave, and he felt a punch to his shoulder from Owen as Alison followed Brady out. Jenny leaned across the island with a look on her face that let him know she couldn't believe what he'd done.

"What?" He gestured to her.

"Mr. O'Connell? Seriously, Ryan, since when are you into formality?" she said, and he didn't miss his brother's laugh and the way he shook his head.

"Since that kid has an interest in my daughter," Ryan said. "As long as he understands the level I'm on and where he is in the pecking order, we won't have any issues."

"You mean as long as you're grinding him into the ground," Owen said, and Tessa laughed.

"If it helps, Ryan, I happen to know that Brady is a great kid," Tessa said.

Suzanne was holding her phone and texting again, standing with Karen.

"You forget he's a teenage boy," Ryan said. "I know what's going through his mind."

Owen laughed outright now, and Jenny shook her head and rolled her eyes.

"Mom just texted back, finally," Suzanne said. "Says she's in a meeting, and it seems she's going to be late, too."

He took in the odd look on Karen's face. So Jack was in a meeting, and so was his mom. "Anyone know anything about Mom having a meeting today and what that's about?" Karen asked.

Suzanne shrugged, and Charlotte's expression turned curious.

"Come on, you guys," Jenny said. "So she has a meeting. Your mom has a life, too, outside you all. She's entitled to do things without you all knowing."

Owen's expression was hesitant, as were Karen's and Suzanne's. Ryan couldn't remember the last time, if ever, that they hadn't known what their mom was doing and where she was.

He heard the door again, then voices, and stepped back to see Marcus, still dressed in his uniform, walking up the sidewalk with Alison.

"Yeah, did she really say a meeting?" Karen said. "Mom doesn't have meetings. That's what she has us for. If she needs something, she gets one of us to do it for her."

All Suzanne did was hand her phone to Karen so she could see the text.

Maybe because of everything that had just happened, with them learning about the secret Owen had held on to about the night their dad had left, Ryan couldn't shake the feeling that there was something more going on. He could feel the way Jenny was watching all of them as if trying to figure out why they were acting the way they were, considering she had no idea of what had happened.

He shrugged and lifted his beer. "So, about Brady, anyone know his last name?" he said, mainly to change the subject before they could talk any further about his mom, which could lead to Jenny wondering more and asking him why they were all so obsessed with what their mom was doing. She would start figuring out that they knew something she didn't—which they did.

Marcus was still outside on the porch, with his daughter, talking. Like, what the hell? Alison didn't do the chatting thing, yet there she was. Maybe he'd pull Marcus aside and get him to find out everything he could about Brady and his father, just to be sure there wasn't a problem there. That was something he wouldn't share with Alison or Jenny.

Jenny walked around the island while his siblings carried on their own conversation, and her annoyance was evident in the way she stood in front of him. "Ryan, if you're thinking of giving that boy a hard time, don't. You know Alison likes him, and you need to get used to the idea that she's going to be dating. I, for one, like him too. So ease up." She poked his chest. "And about your mom, you all need to chill out. She's been there for all of you, every day, for everyone. Whatever she's doing, it's her business. Her business!" She poked his chest again.

He looked back over to Marcus and Alison outside. Whatever she was saying, she was almost smiling.

His sisters were talking with Owen, and Tessa was walking out back now with Charlotte and Eva. Jenny still hadn't pulled her gaze from him.

Okay, so maybe he'd agree, but only after he had Marcus check the boy out.

Then there was his mom and their need to know what was going on. Maybe Jenny was right, considering everything Iris had ever done had been entirely for all of them.

But maybe when she showed up, he'd pull her aside and find out what was going on and who she was meeting with. And maybe that, too, he'd keep to himself.

Chapter Four

"Yeah, Marcus is a big meanie, making Harold work the night shift. You know what that does to a relationship?" Suzanne said, gesturing toward Marcus with her fork before taking a bite of the chocolate cake Charlotte had sent him back over to their house to fetch. She wasn't waiting for dinner. Suzanne had always been about dessert first, as far back as Marcus could remember.

The task had given him a minute to change into blue jeans, a T-shirt, and a hoodie and put his gun in the gun safe in the closet. Marcus knew Charlotte didn't like the fact that he carried it around Eva. When they were home, she wanted him to change and put away the work stuff, even though being a sheriff was who he was.

"He's not working all night," Marcus said, "but we've had a series of late-night crimes, burglaries, thefts. I need him out there. He's one of my best."

He was the best, actually. At times, Marcus thought Harold was an even better cop than him, considering he'd had more than enough personal challenges to pull him away from the job recently.

"Mom's still not here," Owen said, lingering beside him, holding a plate of chicken he'd just pulled off the barbecue. "You know anything about this meeting she had today?"

As Charlotte sent Eva into the bathroom to wash her hands for dinner, Marcus took in his brother. He'd thought nothing of their mom's meeting when Ryan had mentioned it right before asking Marcus to run a background on Brady and find out everything about him, his parents, and his siblings, anything and anyone, all the skeletons in his closet. Marcus was still fighting amusement over his brother's predicament.

"No idea," he said. "I'm sure she'll be here soon, and she can tell us."

Just then, he heard a door close, and Alison called out, "Grandma's here."

"Speaking of…" He wanted to add that his mother was a grown woman with her own life, and they needed to stop worrying—except the fact was that worrying was all Marcus had done since noticing that their mom wasn't there yet. He knew he needed to give his head a shake.

Eva went running to his mom, who stopped to hug his little girl and then Alison, who was sharing some news with her, but the expression on his mom's face had him really looking. Owen rested the chicken on the island along with the salads and the chocolate cake that Suzanne had already cut into.

"Okay, guess we can eat now, or should we wait for Jack?" Jenny asked Karen, who made a face and shook her head.

"No, he said he's in a meeting. If or when he gets here…"

That was all Marcus heard before turning to take in his mom again. She was holding Eva's hand and had her other arm around Alison's shoulders. He couldn't remember his niece ever smiling this much.

Maybe he should take a minute and stop by alone tomorrow to check in with his mom and make sure everything was okay.

Then his phone was ringing, and he pulled it out to see that it was Harold. Charlotte dragged her gaze over to him. He knew what she was thinking: He'd likely have to go and handle something.

"Harold, what's going on?" he said and turned away, touching his mom's shoulder as he walked past and headed out the front door.

"Got a problem," Harold said. "I'm out at old Lionel Shepard's. You know his place, the one that backs onto the forest? He says his dog dug up something, a body. Thought I should let you know before I call everyone in."

"You sure?" Marcus stood on the front porch, hearing the voices in the house. Just then, Jack pulled up in his Mercedes and parked across the street, next to Charlotte's Subaru.

"Not much confusion when it comes to human remains," Harold said.

He dragged his hand over his face. Jack was dressed all lawyerly, in dress pants and a dress shirt. He too was dragging his hand over his face as if he'd had a hell of a day.

"Okay, I'm on my way," Marcus said. "You'd better call everyone in. Get them out there. Find out how fresh it is, and tape it off so no one goes in and tromps around, destroying the crime scene."

The screen door squeaked, and Charlotte stepped out.

"Already on it," Harold said. "See you when you get here."

Marcus pocketed his phone just as Jack strode up the steps.

Charlotte was lingering in the doorway. "You have to go, don't you?"

He leaned down and kissed her. "Afraid so. Lionel's big old mutt dug up a body," he said, and he knew he didn't have to say more. Charlotte understood.

Jack said nothing. By his expression, though, he seemed distracted.

"I'll save you some dinner—and cake," Charlotte added.

He kissed her again as she went in, but Jack made no move to leave.

"Marcus," he said. "I wanted to have a word with you, when you have a moment, about a case. Maybe I can stop in tomorrow…?"

Marcus started down the steps. "Sure, yeah. Give me a call tomorrow. Depending on what happens tonight… Whose case?"

Jack was unsmiling, but then, he couldn't remember the man ever not being dead serious about something. He shook his head. "Tomorrow. I'll talk to you about it then," he said, then lifted his hand as he walked into Ryan's house.

Marcus hurried across the street to grab his gun before heading out to the crime scene. He just hoped that whoever the body was, it wasn't someone he knew. After all, this town was still reeling over the death at the high school, and now someone else? Another body would be one more too many.

THE EVENING WAS FULLY dark as Marcus stood in a clearing in the woods at the boundary of Lionel's property, just before the state park began. There were tarps and headlights, and the crime scene techs were there. The body Lionel's dog had dug up was just bones, but how long it had been there was anyone's guess.

Harold had his jacket on, and Marcus was still wearing his old hoodie, his badge pinned to it, as he spoke with the old man again.

"Told you, Rufus has the hound dog in him," Lionel said. "When he gets a scent on something, he just starts digging. I didn't know what it was. Thought it was just garbage. I was calling him, and by the time I caught up with him, I found him digging up an old tarp. I went to grab him and pull him away when I spotted something. I pulled back what he'd already unearthed and saw the bones. Now, I've hunted all my life, so I know the difference between human and animal. Then I called you all. Someone must've dumped it on my property, buried it. Any idea who it is?"

He just looked at the old man, who had lived there forever. He was a little hunched, a little shorter than Harold, and he wore a worn tan jacket. His wife, he knew, had died twenty years back, and his kids had moved away. Lionel had been known to stir up a mess of trouble in his younger years, having spent the first half of his married life drunk.

"Looks like it's been here a while," Harold said. "It's pretty decomposed. No ID, and dental records are out since the teeth are missing. They'll try DNA, but unless it's already in the system…"

Marcus dragged his gaze back to Lionel. "So you have no idea who this is or could be? I mean, you were known a while back to get into some trouble when you were drinking."

Lionel shook his head. "Look, I wouldn't have called you if this was something I'd done—and I haven't had a drink in twenty-six years, Marcus. I may have done a lot of things, but getting blackout drunk wasn't one of them. I remember every stupid-ass thing I did and said, which I guess is my punishment. You and I both know that in these woods, anyone can do just about anything and not get caught. It's easy enough to get in there, too, with all the trails."

Harold gestured with his thumb to Marcus, and he knew he wanted a word with him.

"Okay, Lionel," Marcus said. "Don't go anywhere, though. We'll likely want to talk to you again, I'm sure."

He turned toward Harold and walked with him toward where the scene had been taped off. A hole had been dug around the body, and the tarp was open, revealing the bones that remained. "What is it?" he said.

"I wanted to talk to you about something the techs said about the body—and about the fact that the DA is here."

That had the hair on the back of his neck spiking. "So what is it that they said?" he asked, taking in the scene and the lights. It was late, and he'd have to wake the mayor soon. Then there was the city council.

He took a second to consider what it meant that it wasn't Eileen, the assistant DA, who had arrived on the scene but rather the big guy himself, Tibo Lewis. That fact alone unsettled him in ways he wouldn't tell anyone. Tibo lifted his gaze to Marcus while talking with one of the crime scene techs.

"The body's been here a while," Harold said. "Anywhere from fifteen to twenty years is their guess. Male for sure, but no ID, as I said."

"So then why is Tibo out here? We have any missing persons during that time?"

Harold hesitated. Tibo said something else to one of the techs before walking his way, and he wasn't sure what this was, but that feeling he had in the pit of his stomach twisted into a knot. He settled his hands on his waist, over his holstered gun.

"Sheriff, was wondering whether I could have a word with you," Tibo said.

Marcus angled his head to Harold, who, he could see, evidently had an idea of what this was about. "What?" was all he said.

Tibo, with his hands in his jacket pockets, appeared far too neat and tidy to be out in the middle of the dirt of a crime scene at night. He didn't pull his gaze from Marcus, nor did he smile. "Want to have a word with you about your dad," he said.

What the fuck?

Marcus nodded, feeling sucker punched. He took in how uncomfortable Harold looked, as if he could feel his walls going up. "We're out in the middle of the woods at a crime scene and you want to talk about my dad? Fuck off, Tibo. That's not your business." He settled one foot in a step toward him and really dug in.

"Well, that's where you're wrong," Tibo said. "When I got the call about a body out in the woods, with no ID, and the right time frame, although sketchy, all I could think was how Rita Mae's lawyer kept carrying on about this knife your brother Owen buried and how you knew about it. All this happened around the time your dad supposedly up and left."

Now he knew exactly where Tibo was going, and for a moment, he had to remind himself to breathe. "That's quite a reach, there, Tibo." He allowed his gaze to flit toward Harold, who said nothing, and it was in that moment that, for the first time, he questioned his deputy's loyalty to him.

"Not when the body is a man's, and the unofficial cause

of death is stabbing. So, again, Marcus, tell me about this knife and Owen's involvement—and tell me, why is it that no one knows what happened to your dad? He was here one day and then gone the next, and no one in town heard from him again."

He had to remind himself to breathe again as he took in Tibo, feeling the situation spinning in the wrong direction. Secrets and lies... He could feel himself on the other side of the law, with eyes on him, twisting things, understanding too uncomfortably well how easily something could be spun against him.

"You know what, Tibo?" he said. "I have nothing to say to you. You want to question me, you do it through my lawyer."

Chapter Five

Jack took his time locking up his car, seeing that Karen was waiting for him beside the BMW he'd bought for her as a surprise one morning after trading in her practical Honda, which had been on its last legs. He'd expected a thank-you or, at the very least, a smile, but what he'd received was two days of silence and her turning her back toward him in bed. That was just something he'd learned the hard way about her. She didn't like surprises.

Or decisions being made for her.

Or anyone messing with her family.

"So you want to tell me what's going on?" she said.

He pocketed his keys and gripped his briefcase, which held all the notes he'd made about Iris O'Connell while trying to wrap his head around her story, her situation. He'd told her not to talk to anyone in the meantime.

Now his wife was waiting for him, and he could feel her seething curiosity quickly turning to anger. Of course, now he knew what she knew, and she hadn't shared any of it with him.

More secrets, a family of secrets. Maybe that was what

bothered him. He'd never expected her to be better at keeping secrets than he was.

"In what sense, Karen?" he said, gesturing for her to keep walking.

She was wearing her trademark dress, a sundress with a sweater overtop, and heels. She made a rude noise, all attitude. Of course, life was never dull with Karen.

He walked with her to the back door of her condo, their condo, and he held the door open for her, but she turned on him in the doorway. She had to look way up, even with heels on.

"Now you're playing games," she said. "You know how I know? You're answering my question with another question. So who was this client you were seeing?"

There it was, the question he wasn't about to answer.

"You know we don't talk about clients and our cases," he said, resting his hand on her shoulder, her back, her ass. Somehow, he had her turned and walking through the steel door, and he closed it behind them and walked with her to the lobby, where she jabbed the button for the elevator.

"You know, that's the thing, Jack. We don't talk about clients and cases because we haven't needed to, not because we just don't. Might I point out there was no agreement not to share information? I'm not asking you to break attorney–client privilege, but we are a partnership. If I need you to handle a motion in court, you go for me, and vice versa."

The elevator opened, and she stepped in and jabbed the button to their floor. The doors closed, and they rode up in silence, both looking up at the mirror in the top corner of the elevator, where he knew the security camera was.

He let her step out first and pulled his keys out even

though she was already rummaging through her purse. He shoved his key in the door and opened it for her.

Her blue eyes held his gaze for a second, and he could see without words that she wasn't going to let it go. She knew something was up, of course. He'd felt it the moment he stepped into her brother's house, and he hadn't missed all the looks from her siblings, the way they were all watching their mom and him.

They were a smart bunch, too smart. He wondered whether they had any idea of the trouble they could all find themselves in if something did hit the fan. He knew well the kinds of things that could happen in the world they lived in.

He closed the door, and Karen slammed her purse on the kitchen island and turned on him. The fire that filled her eyes, he swore, changed the color to a brighter and deeper blue.

"What I want to know, Jack, is why my mother was at the office," she said. "You know, normally I wouldn't think anything of it, but you texted you were in a meeting with a client and were going to be late, and then Suzanne got a similar text saying that our mom had a meeting. Our mom never has meetings. Then Suzanne said that she and Harold saw Mom going into my office—our office," she said, correcting herself and then shutting her eyes for a second. When she was angry, she would say things that were sometimes so damn hard to take back.

He said nothing as he rested his briefcase down on the sofa table and his keys in the oyster dish resting between two lamps. Everything in this condo was hers. She wouldn't have anything of his. He just angled his head, watching her as she fisted her hands in the air, and he could see how worked up she was getting. He wondered whether she'd scream.

"Ah, the silent treatment, where you won't give me anything you don't want to give," she said. "It's not lost on me that the minute you showed up at Ryan's after my mom got there, you said nothing to me about her dropping by, and she said nothing either, which isn't like her at all. It also isn't like her to be so down. She wasn't her same smiling, happy self, laughing with all of us. So I knew then that something was up."

Karen still hadn't taken off her heels. They weren't the low, practical, easy-to-walk-in ones. No, Karen always went high with the kind of heels that gave her those gorgeous legs. She looked so damn sexy even when she was ready to kill him, like now.

"Let me ask you something," he said, not looking away from her. "Are you keeping things from me, Karen?"

She pulled back, confused. "What the hell are you talking about? Why would I keep things from you? And what does this have to do with my mom?"

This was dangerous territory, but he was downright pissed that she'd said nothing. Siblings or not, the O'Connells weren't an exclusive club in which spouses were only guests. If there were secrets, he sure as shit had better know them. "I don't know, Karen. Why don't you tell me about the knife Owen hid, and about how Marcus tried to help him dig it up, and about the night your dad disappeared?"

Her face paled, and her jaw slackened. He crossed his arms but didn't take a step toward her, and she dragged a hand over her face just as her phone started ringing. She reached for her purse and pulled it out.

"Don't answer that," he said.

"It's Marcus," she replied, then didn't look at him as she answered. "Marcus, this isn't a good time... What are you talking about?" Her gaze lifted to his, and her demeanor changed. She rested her hand over her head and pulled it back over her hair, then lifted her palm in the air, a gesture he'd seen from her a time or two when she was trying to make a point. "Okay, listen to me," she said. "You did the right thing. Have they called you in? Did they ask you to leave? What is going on? Oh, for fuck's sake. Yes, go home. Look, I'll be right over." Then she hung up, and he felt, not for the first time, that her family came first and he came second.

"So you know about what happened," she said. "Who told you?"

What could he say? Nothing, so he gestured with his chin to the phone she was still squeezing in her hand. "What was that about?" he said. Yeah, he still wasn't about to come clean. He took a step toward her, and a little bit of the fight that had been in her moments earlier was now gone.

"Remains were found out at Lionel Shepard's. No ID, but it seems you're not the only one who knows about the knife. So does the DA, and he's questioning Marcus right now. They're putting two and two together. Even though there's no ID on the body, and only an approximation of the cause of death, they can determine from marks on the bones that there was a knife wound. The DA asked Marcus to leave the scene, and he wants to see him in his office. He's calling in the sheriff from the county over."

Then she did something he didn't expect. She pressed her hands over her face and started crying.

It took him only two steps to reach her and pull her against him, taking in how well she fit in his arms. She was a noisy sobber, and he pressed a kiss to the side of her head, holding her so tight.

"Well, it seems you O'Connells really painted yourselves into a corner," he said. "Just so you know, you can't handle this case, any of it."

She stepped back, her mascara running. She swiped at her eyes. "Of course I can. He's my brother, and they have no evidence. It's just a body…"

"You mean a body in the woods with no ID," Jack said. "They can spin this into a crime that none of you know for sure even happened."

She angled her head. "You know something, don't you?"

He pulled in a breath and took her in. "Yeah, I do, because your mom came to see me, scared shitless, from what I can figure. It was just a feeling she had that everything she thought had been buried and forgotten long ago was resurfacing. She's afraid of something happening. What, she didn't know for sure. Now, with a body being found, and after hearing from her about the night your dad left… She told me you knew about the knife, the blood, and Owen burying it, and you said nothing to me."

She had a way of not cowering, just something else he loved about her. He reached for his keys.

"What are you doing?" she said, pulling her fingers under her eyes to wipe away the tears and smudges of mascara.

"Time to go see your brother," he said. "He called you, but guess what? It's not you he'll be getting."

Chapter Six

Something about spending time with her grandchildren filled Iris with a joy she hadn't felt even with her own kids, even though she loved them dearly. Raising six kids while neck deep in stress and worry, feeling as if the entire world were against her, she'd never allowed herself time to enjoy the special little moments with her kids, all those times she wished she could go back and redo.

But that was something she wasn't about to admit to anyone. As she carried a slice of chocolate cake wrapped with plastic from Ryan and Jenny's, Eva was holding her hand. Beside her, Charlotte was looking more tired than usual, not yet in her third trimester.

"You know I can stay for a bit, Charlotte, if you want to go and take a bath or relax," Iris said. "Since I didn't get any hang-out time today with Eva…" She glanced down at the little girl, who was now officially Marcus and Charlotte's, legally. Eva smiled up to her and skipped along beside her as they crossed the street.

"You don't have to do that," Charlotte said. "And I

appreciate you carrying that piece of cake, but I could easily have done it."

"Nonsense," Iris said. "I'll tuck Eva in, read her a couple stories, and you can have some downtime. I remember how it was, being pregnant, especially when you have little ones running around. There's a point where you're just so damn tired you can't think straight."

She followed Charlotte up the front steps and waited while she unlocked the door, then followed her inside, taking in the basket of unfolded laundry in the living room and the sound of a car pulling up outside.

She turned in the doorway and took in the sheriff's cruiser. "Marcus is home," she said, taking in her son as he got out of the car. She didn't know what it was, but something in the way he moved and looked around as he closed the door reminded her of a time when he was young and had lost his footing.

"I didn't expect him this soon," Charlotte said, stepping around her to the screen door.

Iris listened to her son coming up the front steps as she continued on into the kitchen with Eva and rested the plate of cake on the island, on which stood a couple of glasses, one with juice, she thought, half full.

"Should we unwrap it for Marcus now?" Eva asked as she slipped onto the stool.

Iris could hear Charlotte saying something to him, but as she stepped back to see the front door, she knew something was off about him. He was looking right at her. "You know what, Eva? You go on upstairs for Grandma and get your pajamas on. Come on, scoot."

She held Eva's arm as she climbed off the stool, and as she strode past Marcus, he rested his hand on his adopted daughter's head and rustled it. She could see that the smile he gave her was forced.

Something was wrong.

"Didn't think you'd be back this soon," Iris said.

Over by the stairs, Charlotte was saying something to Eva. Marcus walked past her and over to the sink, where he pulled a glass from the cabinet and filled it with water before leaning back and drinking it. Charlotte strode back into the kitchen, her eyes big, bold, and worried. She tossed Iris an uneasy glance.

"What happened, Marcus?" she said. "Something did. I know when something is wrong. What happened at Lionel's? You said there was a body?" She glanced over to Iris, who wondered for a minute whether she should leave, because this was the kind of discussion that was between a husband and wife. But something made her feel she should stay.

Marcus lifted his gaze over to Charlotte and said nothing for a second, then over to Iris, questioning.

She knew the look well. "I wonder if I should go and leave you two to talk," she finally said.

"No, Mom. Actually, I'm glad you're here, because I need to talk to you," he said. "Something happened tonight, and it involves you. Because of it, I need to tell Charlotte about the night Dad disappeared."

She thought a strangled sound left her mouth, and he lifted his hand toward her.

"I know you didn't want anyone to know," he said, "but things have taken a turn, and we need to talk about it."

She pressed her hand to her chest. Charlotte didn't say anything, looking up at Marcus before sliding her gaze over to her, her expression shocked. She heard little footsteps on the stairs, and Marcus looked over to his daughter, then to Charlotte.

"Let me just get Eva to bed," Charlotte said before reaching over and resting her hand on Iris's arm.

Iris wondered whether the sympathy in her expression would still be there when she knew the truth about how she'd screwed up so badly. She found herself needing to sit down, and she pulled out a stool at the island.

Marcus stepped closer and rested both hands on the counter, his revolver holstered in his duty belt, which she could see under his old hoodie, just something else that unsettled her. For a minute, they listened to the footsteps on the stairs and Eva and Charlotte's voices, the back and forth.

"So what happened?" Iris said. "I can tell by your face that something did." She ran her hand over the laminate countertop and took in how Marcus seemed so unsure and conflicted.

"There was a body," he said. "There's something you don't know. The woman who saw Owen bury that knife..."

"Rita Mae," she said. "Yes, I'm well aware, Marcus, of the threats she implied and how she tried to use what she saw to save her own skin. We've established that. What else?" She spoke matter of factly, but she couldn't shake the sense that her children were unknowingly being dragged into something she'd never meant them to have any part in.

Marcus nodded. "Yes, but her lawyer added his voice, too. The DA's office heard, but I thought they were paying it no mind until tonight, at the crime scene at the edge of Lionel's property, just in the woods. A body was buried there a long time ago. We don't know who it is, and everything is preliminary, but the DA showed up, and the crime scene techs indicated that the cause of death was likely a knife wound. That could change when they get the remains back to the morgue and do forensics, though," he said.

"I mean, we don't even know who it is or how long it's

been there, but right now, the DA is taking the rumors he heard and the fact that I knew about the evidence Owen concealed, and he's doing the math. It's ridiculous, all hearsay, and what's even more ludicrous is that Tibo brought up the rumors about Dad, about why he left and we never heard from him. He was waiting for me to deny it, but I said nothing. Because we never did hear from him —not a letter, not a phone call, nothing. I heard the rumors, growing up. I remember the cruel things kids said, things they'd overheard from their parents, like that he ran off with another woman, or that he was murdered, and everything in between." He stopped talking for a second.

Iris was trying to wrap her head around what she was hearing. "Are you telling me the DA is automatically concluding that the remains you found tonight are those of your murdered father, even though they don't have any solid information about the date or cause of death? That's quite a reach, Marcus. I'm no lawyer or cop, but I know that much."

She could feel herself lean in, feel the anger surging through her. She couldn't believe what she was hearing, and she knew there had to be more. Marcus just stood there, leaning against the sink, his arms crossed, his hoodie still on, pulled into himself as if trying to figure this out.

"Come on, Marcus," she said. "What is this theory of theirs based on?" She shrugged, shaking her head, sitting up straighter, hoping that Charlotte couldn't hear. Then she realized, in that second, what Marcus was telling her. "It's all come back on you, hasn't it?"

He nodded. "Yeah. The DA wants to question me. I was sent home, and he's called in the sheriff from the county over, yanked my authority away. Harold is still on the scene, and I have no idea where he stands in this. What

I do know is I made an enemy out of the DA when I told him I wouldn't be talking to him without a lawyer."

This was worse than she could've imagined, and for a second, she wondered whether this was why she'd been so unsettled. She'd never been a sensitive person, but lately, she hadn't been able to shake her growing unease.

"I see," she said. "So Harold knows?"

He looked away and pulled in a breath. "Yeah, I had to tell him, and you should know that Karen knows, and Ryan too. We couldn't keep this from them." He lifted his hand as if she were going to interrupt, and she felt that sinking feeling even though she'd already suspected they all knew. "I'm sorry, but we decided without you. I've called Karen, and she's on her way over, and I need to tell Charlotte, because I know what's coming next. They're going to ask me to step back until the coroner can get forensics done and get this cleared up."

She wasn't prone to self-pity, but she felt a world of hurt building in her stomach over what she'd done to her son. "I'm so sorry, Marcus. You shouldn't be involved in this. If I could go back to that night…" She stopped talking, because she didn't know how she could have done things differently when Owen walked downstairs and saw everything—the wrecked office, the destruction, the blood, and her panic.

"Mom, stop. Once the ID comes back on the body and they figure out that it's not Raymond O'Connell, a very different conversation is going to be happening. What gets me is how easy it was for them to create a story without all the evidence. Look, I'm just pissed off because of this reach. This is beyond circumstantial, based on rumor, in a way I've never seen before. But because of all this and all the talk that's going to happen in town, this won't stay secret. Rumors and lies spread, and this will spin a web that will catch a lot of people and ruin a lot of lives. Right now, it's a knee-jerk reaction, but I can't help thinking this was done because someone out there is trying to hurt me, you, Owen, our family…

"After tonight, we need to have a family meeting. We need to tell everyone; otherwise, the blindside could have unforeseen consequences. We need to tell Jenny, Charlotte, Tessa, and Jack, even Alison and Eva. No more secrets. Then there's the letter, Mom, the one you said Dad left. I never asked about it before, but I need to see it."

She heard a car door and had to pull her gaze from her son. Boy, some things he did reminded her so much of Raymond. She heard footsteps, and the door opened, and there were Karen and Jack. She didn't know why, but having Jack there seemed to help.

At the same time, there was no way she was letting Marcus see that letter.

"Karen, Jack," she said. "Marcus was just filling me in." She forced herself to slide around on the stool just as Charlotte came downstairs. For the very first time, she felt as if she were the one in the spotlight, with her life being dissected and every choice she'd ever made coming into question.

"That's great," Jack said. "Because before this goes any further, as I told my wife, Marcus, Iris, and Charlotte, there've been way too many secrets. I want to be clear with everyone that I'm Iris's lawyer."

Marcus was looking at her now, and she wasn't sure what to think.

Jack continued: "Before anything, there are some things I can't and won't talk about, and, Marcus, as I already told Karen, because you're family, she's not representing you. Every one of you will be in the spotlight." Jack took a step closer to her. "I'll be talking to the DA, because until they have an ID on that body, no one is talking to anyone. So call Ryan, Suzanne, Owen, and Luke. I'll talk with all of them. Any questions?"

This was the first time she'd ever seen Karen so quiet.

"Yeah, I have a question," Charlotte said as she stepped into the kitchen, closer to Marcus. She lifted her hand, and Iris could see the confusion on her face as no one said anything. "I don't know what's going on, but I think someone had better fill me in as to what this is, because I'm not liking what I'm hearing. Marcus…?"

Here we go, Iris thought, seeing the way Jack exchanged a look with Marcus, who reached over and ran his hand over Charlotte's arm. She gave everything to her husband, waiting for something.

"No, wait, stop," Iris said. "This is my story to tell." She took in Charlotte, seeing her confusion, and shook her head. "Something happened eighteen years ago to the man I loved, the man I married. I believed him to be someone he wasn't, and in fact, he suddenly turned into a man I didn't know. My children didn't know anything, Charlotte, but Marcus has already pointed out to me that this secret is coming out one way or the other. I think we'd better go sit down, and I'll tell you."

Charlotte said nothing at first, then glanced to Marcus. "Okay, but I have one question," she said. "How long have you known, and how bad is it?"

Jack took a step closer to them. "It's always bad when the law starts focusing an investigation your way," he said. "And it's worse when it becomes a witch hunt, when circumstantial evidence can be spun in any direction. Right now, I want to make sure we're all on the same page. Whatever is said here tonight stays here."

Iris didn't know why she held her breath.

Charlotte shrugged and made a face, resting her hand

on Marcus's arm. "Of course, that goes without saying. We're family. But somebody had better say something, because I'm starting to think some pretty bad thoughts."

Iris fisted her hands and slipped off the stool, taking in everyone. "Let's go sit down," she said, "and I'll tell you everything I know, everything I remember. But just so you know, at that time, I did the only thing I thought I could."

Then she stepped away and started into Marcus's living room, glancing up the empty stairs to where Eva was hopefully asleep. She wondered how long it would be until she learned that her grandmother wasn't the ideal role model she thought she was, and she didn't walk on water. That little girl would no longer look up to her like she did now, as if she could do no wrong, and that thought hurt her more than she could've admitted to anyone.

Chapter Seven

Jack was standing in the doorway of a house that didn't belong to him, taking in the darkness outside, except for the streetlights. His wife was walking barefoot to the kitchen with an empty wineglass, and Iris O'Connell stepped over to him. He took in the headlights from a vehicle coming up the street, and the sound of the engine. It had to be Suzanne, or maybe it was Owen. Both were on their way over after the call Karen had made.

"So how bad is this?" Iris said. She wasn't just his wife's mother but his family, too, he realized. Never once had she made him feel as if he weren't a part of this family. She had always had a smile for him, but no one was smiling now.

"You want me to give it to you straight?" he said.

In the living room, Charlotte was sitting on the sofa, with Marcus sitting on the coffee table in front of her. It seemed there was a heart to heart going on. Then there was Jenny. Apart from her initial reaction of surprise, she didn't seem rattled at all by the news. Why, he didn't know for sure, but at least he wasn't having to deal with anyone who could cause problems and make this situation worse than it was.

"That would be appreciated, Jack," Iris said, sounding unusually calm. She was short like his wife, and he could see how much Karen really did resemble her mom. Iris was holding herself together well, considering whatever had made her come to him earlier that day to begin with now seemed to be unraveling.

"For me to tell any of you not to worry would be ridiculous," Jack said. "There's a wolf at the door, banging to come in, and hearing that Tibo Lewis himself was suddenly at a crime scene, taking serious what Rita Mae and her lawyer were saying about Marcus, how he knew about a crime and covered it up, using his position as sheriff to sit on it as if he's been looking into it all along… I don't know, Iris. The kind of misconduct they're talking about doesn't fly anymore.

"Tibo is obviously wondering whether the accusations could be true, and the unknown body and the preliminary cause of death are confirming his suspicions. A shitstorm is about to land on the doorstep, even if nothing comes of this. It's going to affect everyone in this family, so we need to make sure everyone's on the same page and no one talks to anyone, because I guarantee you, by morning, the spotlight will have shone through the community. There's been an accusation, a bloody knife, but no body until now—and then there's the note."

She looked away. Despite everything she'd shared with him, he wondered how much more there was, and he wondered too whether his worst fear would come true and the ID on the body would prove that it was Raymond O'Connell. If so, this family would be ripped apart in a way he didn't know he'd be able to fix.

"Marcus wants to see the note," she said, her arms crossed.

Owen's plumbing van was out front. He had arrived alone, and Suzanne was there too. No Harold, no Tessa. So this would be it for tonight.

"Yeah, well, tomorrow, you need to show me everything," Jack said. "I'll come by first thing in the morning. You kept everything of his? Where is the note? Because you didn't answer me on that, but I'm sure you didn't toss it. You kept it, didn't you?"

She swallowed.

He took in Owen and Suzanne outside together. Both appeared upset. Whatever they were saying, he couldn't hear them.

"Downstairs," she said. "I had Luke build me some storage shelves. It's in one of the plastic totes where the Christmas decorations are, old photos, some of the kids' things that I never threw out."

Owen and Suzanne were on the steps now, and his wife was still in the kitchen.

"Give me a minute with Karen," he said, gesturing toward her, then ran his hand over Iris's shoulder and squeezed gently, feeling how tense she was. "Listen to me, though. I'm not going to say everything's going to be okay. I won't say that, but what I can tell you is that whatever happens, I've got your back. We'll deal with it."

She nodded and then angled her head toward the kitchen. "Go talk to your wife, my daughter. And, Jack…" she started when he turned to walk away.

He said nothing, waiting for her to finish.

She jutted her chin. "Thanks for coming into Karen's life. I've never seen her so happy, in case I didn't say it."

Then the front screen door opened, and Owen and Suzanne strode in.

Jack walked into the kitchen, seeing Karen over by the sink with a glass of wine, holding it up and swirling it around. He reached for it and took it from her hands. "This isn't going to help," he said, then set it down out of reach on the counter. He opened the cupboard and pulled out a big glass, then filled it with water and handed it to her.

"You're kidding, right?" she said. "Water?" But, to her credit, she took it and humored him.

He thought she was rattled, and he'd seen this kind of uncertainty in her only two times before, both because of him. "I told you before that you drink too much."

"I don't get drunk, Jack. Having a glass or two of wine doesn't make me a drinker." She stared into the glass of water and then lifted it again and took a swallow.

He stood so close to her, taking in the way she pulled in a shallow breath, how the top of her head came up only to his chest. She'd tossed her sweater aside and was standing in just her sundress, which was two shades of blue, a soft stretchy knit that stopped just above her knees. Her breasts moved with each shallow breath she took. He reached for a strand of hair that had fallen free from her ponytail and tucked it behind her ear.

"No, but you have a glass almost every night," he said. "This thing with your family, I love how close you all are, but I can see it in each of you now. It was something I couldn't put my finger on before. You're so close because of what happened, with how your dad was gone and your family as you knew it was suddenly destroyed. You know, with some families, when this kind of thing happens, the family splits, rivalries arise between siblings, and any kind of closeness disappears. They move away and never speak again. But you all seem to have done the opposite and pulled closer."

She flicked her blue eyes up to him. He could see the confliction there, and her strength, and he wondered whether she'd tell him to go straight to hell or maybe walk into his arms. At times, it was a guessing game with her and her fiery personality.

He slid his hand over her cheek and then her shoulder, her bare arm, as she settled the water on the counter.

"I called Luke, and he answered," she said. "I told him he needed to come home." She rested her hands on his chest, splayed out and feeling him. He pulled them down and around his waist as she stepped in closer, her breasts and all that softness pressing into him. He heard the floor squeak behind them, footsteps.

"So you called this meeting. Now what?" Owen said, sounding pissed. He wore a gray hoodie pulled over a blue and white T-shirt, and his blue jeans had a tear at the knee. His dark hair was short but ruffled, as if he'd run his hands through it. "So everyone now knows?"

Karen stepped out of his arms, and Jack leaned back against the counter. Karen was still right there, touching him, and his hands slid around her and held her. "And where is Tessa?" she said.

Everyone was everyone, and from what he'd learned from Iris, he knew that Owen had been the one in the thick of it, the one who had buried the knife, carried the secret, and thought the worst.

"If you're trying to ask whether she knows, yes, she does. Whether I see her again is another story. She was shocked, angry, furious, likely thinking the worst of me."

"Owen, I'm so sorry," Karen said. "Did Tessa really say that to you?"

What was Jack supposed to say?

Suzanne strode in next. "So Harold is working, but you all know that he knows. I tried calling him to see what's going on with the investigation and why Marcus is in the spotlight, but he said he couldn't talk about it." She rested her phone on the counter just as he heard another one ring from the living room, then footsteps outside the front door.

The screen door squeaked and opened, and someone stepped into the house. Owen's face said everything.

"It's Tessa," mouthed Suzanne.

Jack followed Karen and Suzanne behind Owen. The private moment between him and Tessa would be anything but, and Jack took in the distance and the tension.

"You know, Owen, I don't appreciate you walking out the way you did," Tessa said. Her hair was hanging long and loose, tucked behind her ears, and he thought her eyes looked a little red and puffy.

She was clearly well aware that they were all listening, and she looked at all of them, then glanced into the living room, where he could see that Marcus had his phone to his ear and his back to them.

"What did you want me to do, considering what you said?" Owen replied. "'What the hell did you do?' Weren't those your words?"

She pressed her lips together and angled her head, glancing over at him and Karen and Suzanne. "I said a lot of things, mainly because I was furious at you for carrying that secret for so long. You said I was likely going to hear something, and you wanted me to hear it from you first. You're not in trouble, but could you be? I have a right to be angry, and I have some things to say to you, Owen O'Connell, but if you think I would just turn my back on you, then you think very little of me." She was so matter of fact, something about her that Jack liked.

"So what is this, then?" Owen said.

She took a step toward him, and it seemed everyone was holding their breath. "You overreact and think the worst. I had a right to be angry and a right to express it, which I did. Not once in there did I tell you to get the fuck out, but what did you do but walk out the door?"

Oh, she was mad. He took in Karen and Suzanne, who were still standing there instead of going into the living room and minding their business. It seemed that was the one thing no one did in this family.

"But…" Owen started and took a step forward, his expression confused.

"But nothing," she said. "You seem to forget we're in a relationship, you and I. You thought it would be that easy, with you saying you had a secret, something you did, and I wouldn't react to that? Would you do the same if it were me? Come on, Owen. If the situation were reversed, would you turn your back on me?"

The way she asked, Jack wondered how Owen would reply. He knew it would make or break everything he'd built with Tessa.

"Of course I wouldn't," he said. "Why would you even suggest something like that?"

"Because, Owen, you thought so little of me that you automatically assumed the worst about me. I can't and won't have that. I love you, Owen, but right now, I'm so angry at you…"

Owen stepped forward and hugged her, and Jack somehow maneuvered Karen into the living room and gestured for Suzanne, too, because they had now crossed the line and were intruding on something between Owen and Tessa. As he turned away, he heard Owen say in a low voice behind him, "I'm sorry, babe. I'm really sorry."

Jack took in Marcus now, who had hung up his phone. Everyone in the living room was quiet, and he could feel the seconds tick by as if the other shoe were about to drop.

Marcus glanced over to Karen, then lifted his gaze to Jack as he held up his phone.

"I've been called in," he said. "First thing in the morning, I'm to get my ass to the DA's office."

Here we go, Jack thought.

Marcus ran his hand over his head, taking everyone in, and Jack sensed a vulnerability he'd never seen before. It appeared the man was getting his wings clipped, and who knew what else?

"So, Jack," Marcus continued, "as you've pointed out, Karen can't represent me, so meet me at eight a.m. in the DA's office."

No one said anything as he took in this family, his family. Their secret had suddenly become a family crisis, centering on a crime that may or may not have happened. Everyone in the community would soon learn about it and talk about it, and everyone in this family would soon be tested in ways they never had. He didn't think they had any idea how bad it was going to get.

How did he prepare these people, and his wife, whom he loved dearly, for something that happened every day across the country and tore entire families apart?

One step at a time.

"Okay, everyone," he said. "Now it begins."

Chapter Eight

Marcus sat at a table in the DA's office, staring at the flag of his country. He took in Tibo Lewis, the DA, who appeared to have had his hair freshly cut for the day. His gray suit was impeccable, very fitting for his mood, and the expression on his face was one Marcus knew well from when he was talking to a defendant.

"I appreciate you coming in today," Tibo said, gesturing to the spot where Marcus had taken a seat, because he was required to sit.

"As if I had a choice," he replied. He wasn't about to cower to this man, wondering what information he was holding on to, but he'd barely slept all night.

"Nevertheless, I'm sure you're aware of your rights…"

"My client is here willingly, Tibo, so cut the crap," Jack said from where he sat next to him. "He's here to wrap up this witch hunt. But before we start, tell me about the forensics at the crime scene, the ID on the body, the cause of death, and how long it was there. I'm sure you have something, or you wouldn't have called my client, the sheriff, in. That is the reason you have Marcus here, right?"

This was a powerplay from Tibo, as if he were getting ready for something more. "We'll know soon, but I'm not implying that Marcus is involved in any way."

"Yes you are, so cut the crap," Marcus said, though Jack had told him not to take whatever bait the DA came at him with.

Jack leaned back beside him. Tibo was fishing. It was something Marcus understood well. The lies would come next, with Tibo alluding to some evidence they didn't actually have just to see his reaction, and it was damn hard not to react, considering how personal this had become. He could find himself, and his family, under a microscope—as he was right now.

Tibo didn't smile, just made a sound of acknowledgement, as if he'd already convicted Marcus of something. Marcus crossed his arms, leaning back in his chair, feeling the weight of his duty belt and knowing he hadn't yet been stripped of his title of sheriff.

"So tell me about this knife," Tibo said.

"You need to show us the knife you're talking about, Tibo," Jack said. "I'll remind you again, just to expedite this, my client has nothing to say to that, considering you have no knife. Until you have some evidence to link my client to something, move on." He circled his hand in the air.

Marcus was still trying to get his head around the scene out at Lionel's, the body that had been dug up. Considering the decay, he wondered what kind of evidence would even be salvageable after all those years.

"Okay, were you aware of a knife?" Tibo said. "Rita Mae and her lawyer have indicated that evidence was given to your brother, a bloody knife wrapped in a cloth, which she'd seen him bury eighteen years ago. As has been pointed out, your father has never been seen again since. Doesn't that seem odd to you?"

Jack lifted his hand again. "You're getting down in the weeds here, Tibo. Thought I was clear with you that we're not answering. Where's this so-called bloody knife and cloth? It should yield some fiber testing and evidence for you to lean on. It seems the only thing Rita Mae and her lawyer are trying to do is spin attention in another direction to score a deal, and what better way than to accuse the sheriff of misconduct without proof? Or do you have some? Because right now, all you seem to be doing is grandstanding."

Tibo was pacing back and forth, calmly, predatorily. He was holding a piece of paper, but whatever was on it, Marcus had no idea. He would've given anything to see it.

"Hey, Jack, you let me worry about the evidence," Tibo replied. He lifted the paper again, and Jack tapped his pen on his open notepad. Tibo was doing the kind of thing he did when talking with a suspect. There could be nothing, or there could be something, and it was that unknown that always unnerved a suspect, as if the law had the truth the suspect was trying to hide. Marcus had just never expected to be sitting on this side of an interrogation.

"So you're denying there's any truth to what Rita Mae is saying?" Tibo said. "Might I remind you that it's a felony to lie to me, same as to a police officer?"

"As Jack has already told you, these questions are ridiculous and have nothing to do with a case in my county that, as sheriff, I'm handling. You overstepped in pulling me from this case, Tibo," Marcus said.

Tibo remained standing before him. "No, Marcus, I'm right in taking you off the case. Appearances matter. I have legitimate concerns about objectivity."

"Oh, fuck off, Tibo! That's absolute bullshit. I know

how to do my job, and right now, you've overreached. I'm not concerned about appearances. If I were, I might feel differently. By the sounds of it, for you, this is a case you can build an election platform on. What could be better for a DA than the appearance of a dirty cop with deep roots in the community who hid a murder that happened years ago in his family? Can you imagine the scandal and the publicity for you? But we don't even know who the body belongs to."

Jack reached over and squeezed his arm, a warning to shut the fuck up. Marcus just grunted, considering all he wanted to do was shove his fist in Tibo's pale and polished face. He'd never been able to read the man too well.

"This isn't about me, Mr. O'Connell," Tibo said.

So he had been reduced to mister, not sheriff. He wondered whether now was the time to remind the DA who he was.

"Really? Yanking me off an ongoing investigation is overstepping. You have no evidence."

Tibo slid his gaze over to Jack. "Not yet, but we do have a sworn statement. Maybe I should be talking to your brother, Owen."

"Shut up, Tibo," Jack said. "You've got a sworn statement about fuck all, and in jumping the gun like this, you've lost your one opportunity." He slammed his notepad closed. "We're out of here. This visit was a courtesy on our part, but consider that courtesy gone. You keep going on about this bullshit, but let me be very clear: You have nothing, so we're done here." He scraped back his chair and stood. "Let's go."

Marcus followed, his own chair scraping across the worn floor. He knew this room was used often for indictments. He didn't know what to make of Tibo's expression, but something about it said he was far from done.

"Well, that's the thing," Tibo said. "When there's a question of impropriety, a hint of misconduct in the sheriff's department, we have a responsibility to investigate. The community will have my head on a pike if I'm not talking to you, Sheriff, and asking the questions we're all thinking. The night your dad left, something happened. Your dad was never seen or heard from again. And you know what I also discovered?"

Marcus turned back from where he and Jack stood at the door. He knew Jack wanted him out of there now, but he gave everything to the DA, with whom he'd worked closely. Now, being questioned, he felt the weight of the accusation. He was afraid to ask, so he said nothing.

"You have something, Tibo, or is this more games?" Jack said, his hand on Marcus's arm, maybe to stop him from going back into the room and doing something really stupid, like hitting Tibo or saying something that could be used against him and his family.

"Oh, I have something—a lot of somethings and a lot of questions. Raymond O'Connell worked for the railroad, suddenly quit, and your mom never reported him missing. Now, why is that, Marcus? Why would your mom not report her husband missing when she had six kids at home? Yeah, something doesn't add up there. If you add in what Rita Mae saw, with Owen burying a bloody knife that she dug up and kept for all these years, only to give it back to him in a moment of weakness… And you were aware of that. You knew. Now there's a body in the woods, and when the details come back, the evidence, just remember I gave you a chance to come clean. This was your opportunity to save yourself, Marcus."

What was it about the way Tibo was talking that made this feel so much like an interrogation?

"You watch yourself, Tibo," Marcus said. "My father

left because he was too fucking cowardly to stick around. He left my mom to figure it out alone. Don't you start making a crime of that. It's not a crime to walk out on your family. If it were, half the men in this country would be behind bars."

Tibo nodded, and an odd smile touched his lips. "Yeah, but for a sheriff to look the other way when an allegation of a crime is made all because it concerns your family, that's a problem."

What was he supposed to say to that?

"If Rita Mae had come to you, Marcus, about anyone else in the community, you'd have been all over it," Tibo said. "You'd have checked it out. You'd have questioned the person and shone the spotlight deep. You wouldn't have let it go. But you did, because it's your family, your brother, your mother. How many others in your family are involved? Maybe I should be talking to everyone, Karen, Owen, Ryan, Suzanne, and Luke. I'll bring them in and find out what they know about this. Because you know as well as I that when it comes to family, everyone has secrets."

"Let me be very clear, Tibo, in case there's any doubt here," Jack said. "I'm the lawyer of record for everyone in the O'Connell family. This meeting is over. This stunt is done, and the camera and mic you have on will give you nothing when you go back and listen to the recording. You have someone saying shit to save her own skin. That's all you've got. So if you want to have a conversation with any of the O'Connells, your first call will be to me, understand? Because to me, it sounds as if you're trying to ruin the lives of everyone in this family." Jack was curt, direct, and to the point.

"No, what I'm trying to do is follow the evidence," Tibo said. "In case you've both forgotten, that's my job.

And I'm doing my job, not cutting corners because word is already out. You both know how word travels in the community. Everyone is going to wonder why the DA has let this go on, so I have no choice. You're officially on paid leave from the sheriff's office, Marcus. Before you leave here this morning, I'm going to need your badge and your gun."

Marcus knew Tibo was just doing his job, but there was something about the way he'd said it that stung. "Do you have a warrant?" he said.

"Not yet, but we're getting one, and then we'll take your mom's house apart and do the job you should have done."

Marcus stepped back into the room and pulled his gun from his holster. He set it on the table, then pulled his badge off his shirt and tossed it down beside it before striding back to the door, into the hall, Jack moving beside him.

"They're on their way to your mom's right now," Jack said. "You know what the fuck this was? Because I do. He was making sure you and I were busy. If I didn't know any better, Marcus, I'd think they've found something, some evidence. Because in order to get a warrant, they have to have something."

Chapter Nine

I ris pressed her hand over her face and waited for the coffeemaker to beep. It was already late in the morning, but then, she'd fallen asleep after four or five, unable to shake her worries over her family and what they must think of her. She wondered if she'd even be thinking this way if she were acting reasonably, but she couldn't help it.

She thought of that night that she hadn't shared, and now, suddenly, eighteen years of silence was breaking open in a way she never would've imagined. The phone rang, and she considered not answering it, then waited another second for it to go to voicemail.

She reached into the cupboard, pulled out a mug, and poured herself a cup of coffee. Then the phone rang again.

"Oh my God, stop calling!" she said. "I don't want to talk to anyone."

She looked at the ceiling. She needed a minute to get her head together, and talking was the one thing she didn't want to do right now, so she lifted her mug and started into the living room of her quiet house.

She remembered the day Raymond had bought this home. Owen, Karen and Marcus were young, and Ryan had just been born. Three kids and a baby had been crammed into a two-bedroom apartment, and suddenly they had a house.

She flicked open the curtains and took in a sheriff's car parked out front. Marcus was there. So much for her peace and quiet. She'd kind of expected that.

The phone rang again.

"Persistent," she said with a sigh, then reached for it. "Good morning…" was all she got out.

"Iris, it's Jack. I'm on my way there, and Marcus is with me. They're getting a warrant to search your house. Based on what, I have no idea. Listen carefully. They will take apart the house, and if there's something there, they will find it. Understand?"

She looked out the window again, parting the sheers. Looking closer, she saw that it was Lonnie sitting inside the cruiser. She felt time slow as she pulled in one breath and then another.

"I thought Marcus was here, because there's a police car parked out front. I see it's Lonnie. So they're coming…?" She had to rack her brain, thinking of what they might be searching for and what she'd kept. She was still in her nightshirt, wearing only a thin blue housecoat.

"You won't have long if they're sitting out there already," Jack said. "We're on our way there. Remember what you told me last night?"

She put her coffee down, feeling the panic, and it took her another second to remember what he was talking about. "So they're going to search my house, everywhere…"

Another cop car pulled up out front, but she knew the neighbors wouldn't wonder, because Marcus was the sheriff. That was, they wouldn't wonder until they saw her standing outside in her robe and the house was filled with cops. Phones would be ringing, gossip would start, and her life would be dissected again by people who were supposedly her neighbors.

"I'll see you soon," she said calmly, then hung up the phone, thinking of the tote she hadn't touched in years, knowing she'd kept everything she should have gotten rid of. That damn letter was tucked in there when she should have burned it.

She tossed the cordless phone on the chair and started to the stairs when there was a knock on the door, then another.

"Sheriff's office! Open up. We have a warrant, Mrs. O'Connell." The voice was deep, and she knew they wouldn't wait, so she strode to the door and pulled it open, seeing a man she didn't recognize. Lonnie and Colby were there, too.

She was handed a piece of paper, a warrant to search the premises, and she took in the expression on young Deputy Colby's face. He was the one her son babied, and out of the three there, he was the only one who appeared ashamed. Outside, a Mercedes had pulled up, and Marcus and Jack got out of it. All of this suddenly became too real.

"I'm so sorry about this, Mrs. O'Connell, but we're going to have to ask you to step outside," said the officer she didn't know. "We have a warrant to search the house. I'm Sheriff Hodges, from the county over. Again, I'm going to ask you to step out of the house, ma'am."

He was a big man, older, and reminded her of Bert, the sheriff who'd just retired and had been a mentor to Marcus.

"As you can see, I'm still in my pajamas. It's cool out

this morning, and I'm barefoot. Would you mind if I put some clothes on?"

"You can put some shoes on, but that's all," said Lonnie quite rudely, almost cutting her off.

Iris gave everything to the deputy, a stubborn man Marcus had struggled to keep on, not finding the reason he needed to get rid of him. She lifted her chin, openly challenging him to put a hand on her.

"For the love of God, that's my mother," Marcus snapped, cutting across the front lawn. "What's wrong with you? Mom, go and get dressed."

She wondered if the neighbors were watching. Maybe they were. If they weren't, they would have heard Marcus, but it didn't matter, because soon enough, everyone would be talking.

She turned around before anyone could tell her yes or no and started walking to her bedroom, where she closed the door and quickly dressed in the first thing she pulled from the drawer, a pair of track pants and a matching hoodie over her bra and a dark blue T-shirt. She heard the knock the second she pulled on the hoodie, and the door opened. She took in Sheriff Hodges, who didn't look impressed, and it wasn't lost on her how he'd almost walked right in on her getting dressed.

"I'm sorry, ma'am. I'm going to have to ask you to step outside now," he said.

She thought she heard Marcus yelling, arguing, so she nodded. She pulled socks from the drawer and held them up for him to see, then walked past him, out of the bedroom and down the hall, taking in Colby and Lonnie, one already inside the kitchen, going through drawers, and the other in the living room, pulling cushions off the sofa.

She pulled open the front closet door and reached for her sneakers. Marcus and Jack stood just outside the front door, and she realized that the sheriff was standing right there behind her, watching her, as if making sure she wouldn't take anything. She stepped outside barefoot, and both Jack and Marcus reached for her arms. She didn't think she'd ever forget the anger Marcus shot toward the sheriff.

"I'm only going to say this once, Marcus," Sheriff Hodges said, lifting his hand. "You let us do our job. You know the drill, and you know how this works."

Iris sat down on the front step and took in another police car as it parked out front, adding to the chaos. It was Harold, in uniform. He walked across the yard.

For just a moment, no one said anything as she pulled on her socks and shoved her feet into her sneakers. She felt sucker punched because her kids had been dragged into this mess, and now Harold, Suzanne's partner, was here to do his job, but he was also hurting her.

"Make sure they stay outside, Deputy Waters," was all the sheriff said.

Harold took her in, and this was the first time, as she glanced up to him, that she had a hard time meeting his gaze.

"Mom, let's go around back so we're not the focus of the neighborhood," Marcus said.

She still needed to brush her hair, wash her face, have a shower, and brush her teeth. Then there was her coffee, which she'd left sitting inside. She only nodded, and Marcus helped her up. She strode beside Jack, following Marcus, feeling Harold on her heels as if she were a criminal, about to be arrested.

"They were already here by the time you called," she said. "I didn't have time…"

Jack touched her arm. "Not here," he said, his voice low. "Did you have breakfast?"

She took in her patio. Through the window, she could see her kitchen, where every cupboard and drawer was being emptied. Something about it hit her in her stomach, seeing everything that was hers, everything personal, being touched by someone who hadn't been invited in. She felt absolutely, one hundred percent violated. She had to turn and look away.

"You know, Mom, maybe we should leave," Marcus said. "I'll take you to my house…"

"She can't leave, Marcus," Harold said, cutting in. "You know that. You know how this works."

Marcus had never appeared so angry. "So whose side are you on here, Harold?"

She knew she should step in and say something, but she couldn't, considering, for the first time in she didn't know how many years, she found herself struggling not to cry.

"This isn't about sides, Marcus," Harold said.

"Hey, both of you—not here," Jack said, stepping in. He turned Iris away from the house. "You know this isn't helping. Marcus, bring some chairs down over here. Best not to look at what they're doing inside."

Somehow, Jack had her sitting behind the house, looking out at the neighbors' yard. She didn't know whether this was any better, considering they were outside, pointing and looking their way. Of course, they were wondering what she'd done. She knew the news traveled and would be everywhere.

She'd had to hold her head up for years because of the trash talk, and now it seemed it was happening again.

Lord, give me strength.

"Mom, I just called Suzanne," Marcus said. "She's bringing some coffee over."

Jack sat down beside her, but Harold was standing off

to the side. She didn't know what to make of him, and she nodded, then faced him.

"I have only one thing to say to you, Harold," she said. "My daughter is everything. If you hurt her, it won't be my sons you have to worry about. It will be me."

Jack pressed his hand to her shoulder again, likely to stop her, but she was too damn tired and pissed off to listen.

Harold said nothing, so she continued: "You see, in the wild, it's always the mother bear protecting her young, because the male basically fucks off. The mother bear lets you know without a doubt what will happen if you mess with her cubs. She will rip you apart and show no mercy." She let her meaning sink in and took in the way his face flushed.

He shook his head. "No disrespect, Mrs. O'Connell, but I'd never hurt Suzanne. Please, you need to listen to Marcus and Jack and not say anything else," he said. Then he stepped back over to the house.

She wasn't sure what was in Marcus's expression, maybe amusement, and Jack chuckled under his breath. She looked to both of them. "What?" She knew it came out rather sharp.

"Never heard you use the F-word before, Mom," Marcus teased, and for a second she nearly laughed. She would have if the situation weren't so dire.

"I may not walk around cussing the way you all do, but sometimes it's appropriate."

"Well, how about, for your sake, you don't make any more threats?" Jack said. "Harold is still a cop, Iris. It could be used against you."

Marcus was looking over to Harold and then back, shaking his head, which she found odd.

"What is it, Marcus?" she forced herself to ask.

"Don't be so hard on Harold, Mom. Unfortunately, he has no choice. Whether I like it or not, he still has to do his job."

Then came a crash from inside, the sound of something breaking, and she pressed her hands to her face and shut her eyes. She felt a hand on her shoulder and heard Marcus swear, feeling as though everything she was dreading had come another step closer.

Chapter Ten

What was it about getting a text from his brother that made Ryan suspect all hell had broken loose?

He'd been out of cell service for most of the day because of a problem on one of the trails, where a bunch of ATVs had been cutting through private property, tearing up the ground, and basically being a nuisance. It was a pain in the ass that he hadn't been in the mood to deal with, considering the cold shoulder Jenny had given him all night after they got home, all because he'd kept a secret from her that hadn't been his to tell.

Was Jenny angry at his mom? No! She was one hundred percent in Iris's corner. It was him she was angry at.

The result was that he'd gone all hard-ass on a bunch of kids whom he'd normally have given a warning, and now he had a cell phone that was basically blowing up with messages from Karen, Marcus, Jenny… His mailbox was full. What the fuck?

"Shit!" he muttered, dialing the phone as he drove

back into town, feeling grungy and tired, his nerves fried. He was ready to go off on the next person he saw.

"Where have you been?" Jenny answered, starting in on him. "We've been calling all day."

"It's called working, Jenny. I was out of cell service. I have a ton of messages from Marcus and Karen, so what's going on? And before you say anything, I called you first so you wouldn't take my head off for skipping the queue."

Okay, maybe he could've handled that better.

"We're over at your mom's," she said. "Everyone is here. You'd better come, because the police showed up with a search warrant and ripped the house apart. Marcus has been put on leave, his badge pulled. He's no longer the sheriff. Karen said a lot of stuff, basically calling out the DA as a prick. And your mom…I'm sorry, Ryan, but I'm getting really worried, here. I'm concerned about the effect all this stress is having on her."

He heard her sigh, and it took him a second to understand what she was saying.

"Ryan, are you there?"

"Yeah, sorry. I'm on my way. So what made them able to get a search warrant? What am I missing? Did Marcus say anything?" he asked. Maybe he should have talked to Marcus first, but he'd had to remind himself of the pecking order after the cold shoulder of the night before.

He could hear people talking in the background.

"We're all in the dark, but Luke is home now, too. He just got here about an hour ago. Ryan, I'm not kidding when I say they tore the house apart. They went through everything, dumped everything, broke things. Even when the thing happened with Wren…" She trailed off. He knew what she was saying. "They didn't do this."

"Okay, I'm not far. Where's Alison?"

He hadn't told his teenage daughter about any of this yet, because last night, after they'd gone over to Marcus's, Jenny had wanted to wait. Alison had stayed home. Now he knew that was likely the worst decision he'd made.

"She said she was hanging out with Brady after school," Jenny said, "which I thought was just as well, considering what I heard when Marcus called me."

He shut his eyes. After everything that had happened since the day before, getting a background check done on Brady and his family had fallen way down on his list of priorities. "Call her," he said. "She needs to know about Mom now, before it blows up anymore."

There was a hesitation on the other end.

"Jenny…" he started.

"I'll call her," Jenny said. "Just hurry up and get here."

Then she hung up, and he felt that awful, sinking sick feeling as he stopped at a set of lights, taking a second as his thoughts raced to the worst case. What the hell had really happened? There had to be something.

He pulled up in front of his mom's house ten minutes later and could see that Suzanne was already there, as well as Karen, Jack, Owen, and Jenny, their vehicles all parked out front.

As he stepped out of his pickup, he took in Fred Thompson, the neighbor he'd known all his life, watering a bush out front that didn't need watering, staring at their house. When he lifted his hand in a wave, he thought the man was going to walk over and say something, but instead he just ducked his head, gave a passing wave, and turned off the hose and started back to his house.

Ryan found himself taking in the neighborhood he'd grown up in, remembering all too well the whispers from neighbors once they'd learned Raymond O'Connell was gone. The remarks and the looks had stayed with him, and he wondered if he'd ever forget.

He strode up to the house, seeing the curtains were drawn, before opening the front door and stepping inside. He froze as he took in Luke and Marcus righting the sofa. There were cushions on the floor, along with dirt from the plants that had been tipped over, and scattered papers and books . The sofa cushions had been cut open, and feathers were everywhere.

As he walked into the kitchen, he heard Karen and Tessa and what looked like the entire contents of the kitchen drawers and cupboards emptied on the floor, the table, and the counter. Tessa was sweeping up broken glass, and Karen's expression was grim as she held up the handle of a Snoopy mug he'd forgotten his mom still had.

He could hear Marcus down the hall, Luke behind him, going into their mom's room, and Suzanne had pulled out the vacuum. The pictures on the walls were all down and taken apart. This was the kind of mess he'd never expected, and as he walked down the hall, he saw destruction everywhere.

"Holy shit," was all he said as he took in every room. Even the cover for the toilet tank was gone.

In their mom's room, Marcus and Luke were putting the mattress back on her bed. Her drawers had been emptied and her clothes tossed everywhere.

"Want to tell me what the hell happened?" Ryan said. "Like, I don't understand what the fuck this is…" He stepped into the room, and Marcus glanced his way, then Luke, whose new clean-cut hair he would have to get used to.

"Search warrant," Marcus said. "Gave them blanket consent to search everything. They broke a lot and weren't careful. They walked out with some things from down-stairs. What, exactly, I don't know. Mom's down with Jack right now. Of all the days for us not to be able to get a hold of you…"

Luke went to pick up his mom's underwear and bras but stopped. "I'll send the girls in here to fix this up," he said, then stepped out of the room. Ryan wasn't sure he'd seen his brother so off before.

"Sorry, I was in the park with a number of dickheads," he said. "I see you all phoned, so what is this about?" He stepped further into the room, and when Marcus just shook his head, he said, "I'm confused, because last night, if I recall, this was about a crime scene and a body with no ID. Has something changed that I'm not aware of?"

Marcus, still shaking his head, now shrugged.

"And why aren't you more upset?" Ryan snapped. "Because you seem unusually calm."

"Oh, I've had a number of hours to come back down from my blinding rage. Now we need to clean up and put this back together for Mom. For the record, they seem to have something, but I'm out of the loop. The DA asked for my badge this morning, and my gun. I've been put on paid administrative leave while they investigate, which… I'm not sure how a sheriff comes back from something like that. Not sure what else to tell you. Jack is now the official lawyer of record for the family, in case you missed Karen's messages, since the DA indicated he intends to talk with all of us."

Ryan wasn't sure he was understanding correctly as he looked around at the mess. "So they can just do this, just walk in and destroy someone's house and life with no evidence?" he said. He knew he was loud, and he suddenly wondered where Jenny was.

Marcus rested his hands on his hips and sighed, but he said nothing. Maybe he was giving Ryan time to catch up with his ranting.

"Is this the kind of thing you'd do, going into someone's house?" Ryan said.

Marcus made a face and ran his hand over his head, then pulled it back down. "Usually it's specific, the search warrant. Not sure how they got a judge to sign off on this, but it happens."

"And we're supposed to say this is okay?"

"Hell, no!" Marcus shouted, then seemed to pull himself together as he blew out a breath. "It's not okay. And yes, this is personal and intrusive. I've never been on this side of it, and after executing a search, I've never considered for a second what the family goes through, but in all my years of working with the sheriff's office, I saw Bert do this only once, to catch a paedo who was into kiddie porn. Maybe that's why I'm taking this so personally. So, if you don't mind, let's just clean this up."

"Yeah…" was all Ryan got out before Tessa and Jenny strode into the bedroom.

Jenny hesitated only a second before going into his arms so he could hug her. When she pulled back, he took in Tessa, who was already picking up clothes. Marcus had walked out of the room.

"I called Alison," Jenny said. "She's coming over. She may as well pitch in, and then we'll fill her in. Your mom is downstairs with Jack. You should go say something to her."

He just nodded, then gestured to the clothes. Tessa was picking up a jewelry box that Ryan had given his mom for Christmas when he was just a kid. The side was broken, and he had to turn and force himself to walk away, out of the bedroom, down the hall.

When he heard the front door open and in walked Harold, he wasn't sure what to say.

What he didn't expect was for Suzanne to walk over and slap him.

Evidently, he'd missed a lot more than he realized.

Chapter Eleven

Beside Iris, Jack had rolled up his sleeves and was standing with her in the circle of mess. On one wall in the back, where boxes had been stacked neatly, everything had been pulled down and dumped. In Raymond's office, which she'd long since turned into her yoga and exercise room, with a stationary bike she'd used just once, she couldn't step anywhere without kicking something.

She bent down and picked up art supplies scattered from their brand-new box, meant to be a gift for Alison for her upcoming birthday. What hurt more than anything was the fact that someone could come in and rip apart something that was so personal and special for her with no thought or care.

She still needed that shower, and then there was her hair. She hadn't taken the time to search for her hairbrush in the disarray, and seeing all of it had her feeling violated in a way she didn't think she could've explained to anyone.

Jack was lifting the boxes back into place, but she knew the police had walked out with the plastic tote in which she'd kept some things from Raymond's office, their wedding photos, his files, and that damn letter.

Why had she kept it? To torture herself.

"So what happens next, Jack?" she said, having to clear her throat when it caught. Her back was to him, and she was still holding the art supplies, the broken charcoal and pencils and the torn canvas. She could hear him lifting another box back onto the shelf.

"We clean up and wait for a call," he said. He was so matter of fact, and she found herself turning to the man her daughter had married, to whom she was looking to save all of them.

"And what kind of call is that? I sort of know, but just to be clear, don't hide anything or sugarcoat it, because it won't help me if you do that."

He just nodded before they heard a commotion upstairs—yelling, she thought, from Suzanne. She glanced once to Jack before jogging up the stairs, him behind her, to find Harold in the doorway and Marcus holding back a spitting-mad Suzanne. There was a red handprint across Harold's face. She stepped into the dining room and living room, where everyone was standing, watching.

"You lied to me! How could you be here and do this to my mom?" Suzanne screamed. "And then you left with that prick of a sheriff and Lonnie. Marcus, you should have fired him when you had the chance! Now look at this."

Iris just took in her daughter, who was so over the edge with rage, and then glanced over to Alison, who had just walked in the front door. She stood there, wide eyed, and Iris realized she was still holding the art supplies. She put them on the dining room table, which was covered with dishes from her cabinet, and gestured for Alison to come over.

When she did so, Iris slipped her arm around her shoulder, not giving a second thought to the fact that she was wearing a short skirt and white tank top, with a jean jacket overtop.

"Grandma, what's going on here?" she said. "What happened? Was there a break-in?"

She wished it were that simple. She wondered if she'd have felt less violated in that case. "Oh, I'm afraid it's more than that," she said, trying to force a smile as she rested her hands on Alison's shoulders and rubbed. "Something that happened a long time ago is coming back on me…"

Ryan was coming her way, and Jenny was standing just to her side, her expression relaying the same shock that Iris was numb with.

Harold lifted his hand to his face, to the red handprint, which had to be courtesy of Suzanne, and no one said anything, which just made everything that much worse.

"Suzanne, calm down," Marcus finally said.

Luke had stepped further into the room, and Jack reached for Karen, who was in sweats and sneakers, and pulled her back, because it looked as if she wanted to go a round with Harold, as well. Harold still said nothing and was standing with his hands over his duty belt. Before, he'd seemed like family, but now he was so official, and it terrified the hell out of her.

"Can we talk?" Harold said, looking right at Suzanne. "I understand you're upset…"

Suzanne lifted her hands, brushed off Marcus, and stepped back. Ryan too was staring at Harold. She glanced back over her shoulder to see Owen and Tessa, who both took her in. The only ones missing were Charlotte and Eva, and there was no way she wanted either here for this.

"Upset?" Suzanne said. "No, I'm not upset, Harold. I'm a little past that. I'm furious. This morning, when I showed up with coffee and tried to talk with you, what did you say? You asked me to go stand over by my mother and Marcus and Jack, because I couldn't interfere. That was what you said to me, you know, your girlfriend, your partner, the woman you live with. So now I'm suddenly…" She was shaking her head.

For a second, Iris thought it might be best to shut the conversation down, but she was just as angry and wanted to hear his explanation. How could he?

"This isn't all on Harold, Suzanne," Marcus said, standing with his back to Harold, looking so damn tired.

"Suzanne, look, this isn't personal," Harold said. "Let me be clear: This was happening with or without me today, and just so you know, I only got wind of it after the warrant was served. I never had any advance warning. This entire shitshow took place around me, leaving me completely out of the loop, likely because they believe I'll say something and be the weak link." He didn't pull his gaze from Suzanne, giving everything to her, before taking in all of them, his expression grim.

"What do they know about the body?" Marcus asked. "Do they have an ID? Come on, this is unbelievable. The warrant here was an overreach, Harold. What do they have? What did you tell them?"

The way Harold stared right back at Marcus, Iris saw something that could break her family apart.

"If you're asking whether I said anything about what you shared, I was clear that I have your back," Harold said. "But going forward, I've already been summoned to the DA's office, and just so you know, Lonnie Bush was officially appointed acting sheriff an hour ago over me because of his time here, his seniority, and, as far as they're concerned, his impartiality and lack of favoritism toward you. They've determined the skeletal remains are male, in his forties, and, based on the degree of decomposition, he's been dead for fifteen to twenty years, falling within the time frame of when Raymond O'Connell disappeared. They know the fatal injury was a knife wound. There's enough tissue for a DNA sample, but there're no matches in the system."

For a moment, Iris thought he was going to tell them more about this insane case, but Suzanne stepped toward him, her hands gesturing and her expression pissed. "That's it?" she snapped. "What they did to my mom's house is because of some corpse that was dug up? They're saying it's our dad, yet they can't determine that, and this whole thing is based on that mouthy bitch, Rita Mae, and her lawyer, who are trying to spin something here…"

"It's not that simple, Suzanne," Harold said. "The problem is that Rita Mae gave a sworn statement in great detail about the night Owen was seen burying something, which she dug up because she was out there. The seed was planted in the DA's mind, and you can build a case on anyone with enough circumstantial evidence. They want your mom brought in…"

Iris felt the ground soften, hearing her sons all talking, shouting, yelling. All she could do was hold her grand-daughter, who was staring up at her, freaked out, and she felt someone's hand on her shoulder.

"Grandma, what's going on?" Alison said. The emotion in her voice cut right to Iris's heart, and she opened her mouth to say something, but nothing came out, so all she could do was shake her head.

"On what charges?" Jack finally said, cutting in. He, Marcus, Luke, Ryan, and Owen had suddenly formed a wall, as if they wouldn't let Harold pass or get anywhere near her. It was with horror that she took in the disarray, the destruction.

"It was me she saw burying a knife, yet they're leaping to my mom?" Owen shouted.

"The problem is that your mom didn't file a missing persons report, and, I shouldn't be saying this, but they're basing this investigation on the argument that a reasonable adult would have called the police to report your father missing. Everything here is circumstantial, yes, but they're of the mind that Owen was just a minor. You should know you could be brought in next, though. Right now, they're bringing Iris in because they found something during the search."

Her heart was pounding, and she wasn't sure if she'd ever get the shock on her kids' faces from her mind.

"And what did they find?" Jack said, then turned to her. "Iris, say nothing."

"They found enough that they want Iris brought in," Harold said. "They found a letter with dried blood on it, and the DNA they were able to get from it was a match to the remains. That's all I know."

Everyone was looking over to her, and she racked her brain.

"There was blood on it?" she said, looking over to Marcus, Luke, Karen, and then Jack, who strode over to her and put a hand on her shoulder.

"You say nothing, nothing at all," he said. "No one talks to you."

There was still arguing going on behind him. Her house was an absolute shitshow.

She heard Harold yell, "You think I want to bring her in? No! I said hell, no! But it was either me or Lonnie. Do you really want Lonnie bringing your mother in? Because I don't. You know he's got a chip on his shoulder where you're concerned, Marcus, and anything in that ride to the station could be used against your mom. Evidence could suddenly appear, or he could say she suddenly started talking."

She could see her sons weren't going to move.

"Marcus, Owen, Ryan, Luke, stop," Iris said. "He's right."

Suzanne moved over to her, and Alison was suddenly standing with Jenny, crying with her arms around her mom.

"Mom, this is absolute bullshit…" Suzanne said.

"I know, Suzanne, but arguing and fighting isn't going to help. Jack will get me out, all right?" she said before dragging her gaze over to Jack, who was already rolling down the sleeves of his dress shirt.

"I'm right behind you," he said.

She stepped forward, and Harold moved around Marcus. She took in the cuffs in his hand and thought her knees were going to give out on her.

"You're not cuffing my mother," Marcus said. "Let us bring her in ourselves."

She could see that the young man her daughter loved was between a rock and a hard place.

"I'm sorry, Iris," Harold said. "It's the law. I'll let you keep your hands in front."

She only nodded. She could hear everyone talking to her, to Harold, but feeling the bite of the cuffs on her wrists made the world fall into slow motion.

He read her her rights, and she thought she said yes to whatever he was asking. Then she felt a hand on her arm, Harold's, and then another on her back and her other arm, her kids', as she was walked out of the house.

She took in the neighbors watching from across the street and likely next door, too. Right, this would just be another nail in her coffin, and this time she didn't know how she'd be able to hold her head up.

Harold opened the back door of the cop car, with the bars and mesh, and helped her into the cramped back seat. He stood there for a second and leaned down. "I'm really sorry, Iris. Just listen to Jack, and don't say anything. Keep your head down, because even though it's not that late, it's late enough that you'll be in jail overnight. It won't be comfortable, and everyone will be listening to anything you say."

There was something in his blue eyes—a warning, she thought. She only nodded, and he closed the door and walked around the cruiser. She looked out from the back-seat, where criminals sat, seeing her children outside, her family. Jack was walking to his car as Harold pulled away from the curb, and all she could think was to ask herself why she had kept that letter.

Damn Raymond O'Connell!

Chapter Twelve

"I want you to stay home," Marcus said. "I told you before, we'll figure it out."

Charlotte was pulling her deputy uniform on over her very pregnant belly, and he strode over and touched her hands over the buttons, taking in how tired and stressed she looked. He was aware of how little she'd slept the night before.

"I have to go to work," she said. "I'm likely to be sent back home, and you know that, but I have to go, Marcus. I think it's important I'm there. At least I can get an idea of what's going on with Lonnie in charge. I'll have a heads-up on whatever he's planning or whatever evidence comes in on the case. I still can't believe he was appointed..." She shook her head and then sat on the bed.

She went to reach for her sturdy shoes on the floor, but he bent down and got to them first, holding each up so she could slip her foot in. He tied one for her and did the same with the other as he looked up at her, wishing he could fix all of this.

Just then, Eva came into the bedroom, holding a doll.

That wasn't something he'd seen her do before, but he knew she was picking up on their stress.

"Hey there, sweet pea. You're not dressed," Marcus said.

Eva was still in her pink pajamas, and he lifted her so she could sit on the unmade bed beside Charlotte. "Marcus, how come I can't go to school today?" she said.

He knew she loved school, but with everything happening, the talk, the gossip, he knew well that someone would say something about her grandma and about him, and he wasn't about to take that chance.

"Alison is staying home, too," he said. "Think of it as a party day, a fun day. There's some adult stuff going on, and I would feel better with you staying close to home."

"Is Grandma going to come over? I didn't see her yesterday."

He stood and wrung his hands, because he needed to get going to meet Jack and everyone at the courthouse. His mom had been locked up for the night, and he was still sick, thinking of the hard bench and crowded accommodations at the county jail.

How could the blood on the letter she'd kept match the remains on Lionel's property? This was his mom, so how could he come to terms with the fact that evidence he should've known about was coming together against her, and he didn't have a clue how to fix it? It was one of his worst fears.

"You'll see her tonight," he said. "Now go get dressed, because Alison will be here soon." He forced a smile, and Charlotte pressed a kiss to her bed hair as she slipped down and strode out of their bedroom.

"Marcus, will she get out?" Charlotte asked.

"Of course she will. Jack's good, and the case is…"

"I know, Marcus, but you and I both know that

anything can happen in that courtroom, depending on who the judge is and what the DA is coming at her with. Do you even know what they have on your mom? You said something about a letter she kept, how they were able to get enough evidence off it to match it to the body." She let out a sigh. "Is the body your father's?"

She was asking everything he'd been thinking, but he didn't know what to say to her, because he was still reeling over what Harold had said. Jack had talked to them only briefly before going radio silent, and when Marcus had tried to call him the night before, Karen had answered and told him quite pointedly that her husband was busy getting ready for the next day.

"I don't know," he said. "I guess I'm just having a little trouble with all this."

Charlotte stood up and rubbed her hand over his chest, over his dress shirt and jacket. He couldn't remember the last time he'd worn a suit. Good thing it still fit.

"Well, you'd better get going," she said. "You don't want to be late. Don't worry about Eva or me. What's the worst that could happen? If they fire me and send me home, then I guess I'll join the ranks of the unemployed."

He knew she was trying to make light of this dire situation. As she walked down the stairs ahead of him, he heard a knock at the front door, and he stepped off the last step, around Charlotte, and pulled it open to see Alison. Ryan was behind her, freshly shaved, already dressed in a dark suit and tie as well.

Alison walked into the kitchen with Charlotte, and Marcus just took in Ryan. For a minute, he didn't know what to say, considering Karen had called each of them and said to wear their Sunday best for their mom.

"Jenny's coming too," Ryan said, letting the screen

door close behind him. "She's just locking up the house. We'll take her Jeep."

Marcus just nodded and then started to the kitchen, but Charlotte was already walking toward him with a go mug of coffee. He took a second and let his gaze linger, then leaned down and kissed her. "Thank you," he said in a low voice as she reached around and ran her hand over his lower back and his butt, then up.

"Yeah, tell your mom..." she started, but she didn't have to finish.

"I know." He rested his hand on her shoulder and looked past her to Alison, who, it appeared, had helped herself to coffee. He could hear Eva on the stairs saying something to Ryan, who was waiting.

"Don't take any crap from Lonnie, you hear?" Marcus said. "He does anything, and I mean anything..."

She reached over and pressed her hand into his chest. "You need to go. And don't worry; I've worked with Lonnie a long time. I know his crap. It'll be fine. Stop worrying."

He kissed her again and started to the door just as Eva strode past in her pajama shirt and shorts, half dressed. "See you later, squirt," he said and rustled her hair, then stepped out of the house with Ryan and let the door close.

Across the street, Jenny wore heels and a skirt, with her jacket pulled on overtop. Her dark hair was hanging long and loose. She lifted her hand, opened the back door, and slid in. Ryan had the keys ready.

"Jenny, I can sit in the back," Marcus said.

"No, Marcus, it's fine. I'm already back here," she said as she pulled the door closed.

He didn't say anything else as he slid in, and Ryan started the Jeep and backed out of the driveway. Charlotte was just leaving the house, walking to her Subaru, and she lifted her hand in a wave.

"She's going to work?" Ryan asked, though it wasn't really a question.

"She has to," was all he said. He glanced back to Jenny, who didn't offer him a smile, because there was nothing about that day that anyone could find any joy in.

They parked behind the courthouse, and he saw that Karen and Jack were already there with Suzanne and Luke, and Owen and Tessa, as well. The three of them joined the group.

"Has Mom arrived yet?" Marcus said.

Jack was dressed in a black suit, white dress shirt, and gray tie in a shade that matched his eyes. It was the kind of thing he hadn't noticed before, how Jack was always impeccably groomed. He held a briefcase, and his expression was all business.

"Not yet, but she will be soon," he said. "I checked in with her already. Harold will be bringing her."

"How is she, Jack?" Suzanne said. She wore dark pants and a white shirt with a jacket overtop, and her hair was in a ponytail.

"She's tired but unbelievably strong, and she told me to tell you all not to worry, though I could tell she was putting up a front. Now, I've already talked to Karen about this, even though she's a lawyer. This is your mom, and, Marcus, I know you've been through this and know what to expect, but not from this side, you haven't. None of you have.

"From this moment on, whatever happens in there, whatever is said, show no emotion. This is important, and I need you all to be on the same page, because everyone is watching all of you. If you smile, it'll tell everyone this is a big joke to you, or if you get angry, people will see arrogance. They're looking for confirmation that your mom is guilty, that you're all guilty, that you did something eighteen years ago and you all knew about it, so you all hid it.

"No reactions at all. Do not answer questions, and do not look at the reporters. Keep your heads high and your expressions free of any emotion, like you're playing a game of poker. Get your game face on, all of you. This is for your mom," Jack said.

Marcus wanted to pull him aside and ask him a ton of questions, but now wasn't the time.

"You all know how this works," Jack continued. "You need to ignore the rumors that are being spread, all of them. They'll be vicious. People are looking to get a reaction out of you. I can't say enough how much of a media frenzy this is going to be, considering who you all are in this town. Marcus, Ryan, Owen, Luke, Suzanne, Karen…" He let his gaze linger on his wife for a second before lifting it back to them. "Don't react, don't respond, don't talk. Eyes forward. Let's get your mom out. Ready?"

Karen slipped her hand around his arm, his hand gripping his briefcase, and they all fell in behind as they walked around the building, to the front, where there were three news vans and more people than he'd expected. Cameras flashed, and microphones were shoved in his face, questions being shouted, asked, called out.

All he could think as he walked into that courthouse was that he'd been there so many times with suspects, but on the other side. So this was what it felt like to be on the wrong side of the law.

Chapter Thirteen

The courtroom was packed, the bailiff standing in the corner. The judge was Thompson, so at least Jack had that on his side, as the man was a stickler for propriety. This was just a preliminary hearing to get bail, but that wouldn't stop Jack from attempting to have the charges tossed out.

He stood with everyone as Iris was led in, wearing her clothes from the day before, her hair sticking up. He heard Suzanne gasp behind him and whisper, "Mom…" He didn't glance back but hoped Karen could keep everyone in line.

Iris forced a smile as she was led to the table and sat down, and he instantly put his arm around her back and leaned in.

"Just follow my lead," he said. "Game face, like I told you."

The court clerk read off the charges: "Murder in the first degree."

He had known that was coming, but he'd expected more—evidence tampering, body tampering, something.

"Is the district attorney's office ready?" Thompson asked, and Jack didn't have to look over to know that Tibo Lewis, who was there alone, was confident as he stood and buttoned his suit jacket.

"Yes, Your Honor, the state is ready."

"Very well. Defense, how does your client plead?"

Jack scooted back his chair and helped Iris up, as well. "Not guilty, Your Honor."

"I take it you'll be asking for bail?" the judge asked.

Jack sat back down and rested his hand on Iris's back again, feeling how tense and shaky she was. "Yes, Your Honor, we will."

"Very well. Let's hear the bail arguments." The judge wore thick glasses, looking out at Iris and then over to Tibo, who stood again.

"As you well know, Your Honor, the defendant's son, Marcus O'Connell, is the sheriff in this town, and the defendant's other children are people we all do business with in the community and have fond feelings for. Even I am empathetic to this situation, but it's been alleged that the sheriff, who has been asked to take a leave of absence during this trial, used his position to conceal evidence in a crime to protect his mother and brother and used his authority to manipulate that evidence—"

"I'm sorry, Mr. Lewis, but Sheriff O'Connell is not on trial here," the judge said, cutting in before Jack could stand to object. "Do you understand that, or do I need to outline the charges and who stands accused?"

"Of course, Your Honor," Tibo said. "…But if I may, the sheriff and his influence in this case have great relevance regarding the motion for bail. All the O'Connell children have positions in the community. Luke O'Connell is with the special forces, Ryan O'Connell is a park ranger and had access to the crime scene on park lands, and Karen O'Connell is also—"

"You Honor, my client's children are not on trial here," Jack said. "This smear campaign is nothing more than a blatant attempt on the DA's part to spread rumors in a community that's ready to go off like a powder keg. This is character assassination, and this case, too, is nothing more than a witch hunt based on a story. The evidence is merely circumstantial, and the warrant that was served—"

"This is just a pre-motion hearing for bail, Mr. Curtis, so save your indignation, as we're not going to argue the evidence in this case," the judge cut in, peering over his glasses to Jack and then sliding his gaze over to Tibo as if to make a point. "That will be taken up at trial, which will be set for two weeks from today. Mr. Lewis, again, I've already made it clear that you're straying into dangerous territory. Iris O'Connell is the one on trial, not the O'Connell children."

"Of course, Your Honor, but as I said, this has relevance on bail."

The judge waved his hand. "Make your argument then, Mr. Lewis."

Tibo pulled out a piece of paper from his folder. "The state is asking for bail in the amount of two million in cash and five million in bond based on the severity of the crime and the lengths the defendant went to conceal the crime with her children—"

"This is ludicrous! Are you kidding, Tibo?" Jack cut in. "I've never heard of such outrageous amounts."

The look the DA tossed his way was anything but friendly. It was all business. They were adversaries in battle, fighting to win at all costs. "As I said, Iris O'Connell is accused of murdering her husband, and, based on the evidence, we believe she will be a flight risk. Her children have the means, contacts, and knowledge to see that she flees the jurisdiction, considering the overwhelming likelihood of a conviction. The state will be seeking the maximum of life in prison with no chance of parole. Based on this alone, we also ask that the defendant be fitted with a monitoring bracelet and confined to her home until trial."

Jack could hear whispers behind him, outrage from Owen, and an F-bomb, he thought, from Luke. "Your Honor, my client is not a flight risk," he said. "She's the mother of six grown children, with grandchildren, and another grandchild on the way. She has deep ties to this community, where she raised her children, and she has a modest income from a pension. She has no priors, Your Honor, not even so much as a parking ticket. She has no access to that kind of cash."

"The court does not consider Mrs. O'Connell a flight risk in the least, Mr. Lewis," Judge Thompson said. "At the same time, this is a murder charge. Taking into account no priors, bail is set at five hundred thousand, with two hundred and fifty thousand posted in cash." The judge took in Iris beside him. Even to Jack, her face seemed pasty white. The judge shook his head. "And I see no need for a monitoring bracelet. The trial is set for two weeks from today and will be assigned to Judge Anderson."

As the judge banged his gavel, the bailiff was at the table, his hand on Iris's arm.

"Go," Jack said to her, rubbing her arm. "I'll see you out there. This is just procedure. We'll post bail and have you home."

As she was led away, he turned to his wife and her siblings, this band of misfits that was his family. He could see Marcus's outrage and the emotions on their faces. Of course, they all wanted to say something.

"Let's go post bail and get your mom out of here," he said. "We'll have time to talk after. Remember, poker faces. Say nothing, no matter what. There's cameras and reporters, people out there you thought were friends, and every one of them will suddenly have a story about you. Hold your heads up. Get your mom home. I'll see you over there."

As the rest of the O'Connells filed out of the courtroom, Karen looked at him with agony in her blue eyes.

"That's a lot of money, Jack," she said. "I have about one hundred in cash…"

He rested his hand on hers. "You and I have the cash. We'll post it. But, hear me, it's only going to get worse, and you know it. You're used to it as a lawyer on the other side, not with an entire town coming at you."

She shut her eyes for a second and pulled in a breath, and he could see the toll this was taking. "One step at a time?" she said, and he wasn't sure whether it was a question.

"Yeah, let's go," he replied.

As he walked out of the courtroom with his wife to where bail would be posted, where Iris would be released, he thought of how this was quickly becoming a circus. He wondered, did they have any idea what they were in for?

Likely not.

Chapter Fourteen

He knew it had been a mistake to come back, even though something about Livingston had been calling him for so long.

He took in his son in the family room by the old brick fireplace, a room with an old shag carpet that he'd been planning on ripping out, and the girl sitting beside him on the dated sofa that had come with the house.

He could hear the video game, the blasting of guns, as he looked down from the kitchen into the family room of the sparsely furnished house. He hesitated only a second, taking in everything about the teenage girl, Alison. Her dark hair and eyes were a different shade than his son's, but she had the same shape of face as Brady.

The fact was that her family was going through the worst thing imaginable.

He shoved in his earbuds, taking in the news playing live from the courthouse on his iPhone, a broadcast about the murder trial of Iris O'Connell.

He'd watched her, seeing her short dark hair, her round face. Iris was a woman he'd never forget. He wondered if he could've picked out the kids, who were now grown. Their faces were down, the cameras were flashing, and the people circled and crowded around the family as they left the courthouse.

The lawyer was Jack Curtis, whom he knew was married to Karen, who was the image of a young Iris. The reporters called out to Iris, to Marcus—to Owen, the eldest. He admired their restraint, considering they'd have had every right to knock those vultures to the ground.

He willed them to do it, but at the same time, he knew they were doing everything right.

"Alison, what time do you have to be home?" he called out, looking down. The kids didn't pull their gazes from the video game at first, but then Alison did.

"I don't know," she said. "I haven't heard when they'll be home." She gave that teenage shrug she did anytime she was uncomfortable. It was just something about her he'd noticed.

That was all she said, even though he'd listened carefully to everything she'd said to his son. Her aunt Charlotte had arrived home an hour after leaving that morning, saying she had time off, but Alison knew she'd lost her job. Her parents weren't letting her go to school because of what people would say about her grandma, her family. They didn't want her hearing the trash talk.

She wasn't supposed to talk about what had happened, but she openly wondered with Brady about whether her grandmother had in fact killed Raymond O'Connell, her grandfather. Maybe that was why he hadn't been able to walk out of the kitchen and leave the two of them alone.

He wondered what Ryan would think if he knew what his daughter was speculating about Iris. The girl didn't hide the fact that she loved her grandmother even though she wondered whether she was guilty. It seemed one didn't cancel out the other. Alison was lost, troubled, he could see, and looking to bend Brady's ear. She'd walked to the park that afternoon and waited for Brady to get out of school, and he'd brought her there after hearing the rumors spreading, the gossip that fueled public scrutiny over the O'Connell name.

There was just something about his son. Brady had a soft spot for the down and out. He took after his mother that way.

He replayed the news from a different station, a different camera angle on the O'Connells as they surrounded their mother. He watched as they climbed in their cars to leave the courthouse, and he wondered for only a second whether he should tell Alison that they were on their way home.

An email popped up on the screen, confirming the booking he'd made to Barbados, the cottage on the beach, all white sand. The tickets had been paid for. His son's school wouldn't be notified. Tonight, he'd tell Brady.

Playing with fire was one thing, but being stupid and careless was another. And he had been so careless only one time before.

"Brady, don't forget you have that report due in your history class," he said.

He didn't look up but could hear Alison whisper something to Brady with her teenage attitude. The fact was that she was sitting too close to his son. Then there was the low-cut shirt, her body too much like a woman's. His son had eyes for the girl, and he couldn't let that happen.

"Did it already, Dad," Brady said, as if he were just a passing thought. "Scored!" He put down the remote. "You want to head out to the park?" he said, turning to Alison.

Ray lifted his gaze to his son, seeing how much he liked this girl, who was Ryan O'Connell's daughter. He'd seen

Ryan only once from a distance, and there was something about him. He could see himself in him at that age.

"Don't be long," Ray said, taking in the way Brady grabbed his jean jacket and pulled it on. He strode to his son, as Alison was already at the front door, bending over, tying her shoes. "No funny business," he said. "She's going through a rough time, and you know what I mean. Hands to yourself, no matter what." He knew his son understood.

"I'm not a jerk, Dad," he said.

Ray took in his teenage son, who was going on eighteen but had been held back a year. He knew Brady wasn't telling him everything. "No, you're a teenage boy with hormones, and that girl's family is falling apart. I'm serious. Don't be a dick. Let her talk, but that's it. Be home in an hour." He lifted his watch. "I have some things to do, someone to meet, so start the burgers if you're back before me."

"Fine," Brady huffed out.

Ray followed them to the front door, still stuck on the minute Brady had walked in with Alison, bringing her to their home, this temporary place he'd planned to stay longer. He wanted to remind his son of what he'd said: "Don't bring anyone over." Yet Brady hadn't listened. Here was Alison.

Above everything else, the fact was that Iris was in trouble, and he'd left her too many years ago to save her now.

He listened to the door closing. He'd put a deposit on this place, having paid for four months, along with the promise to work on the house, but he knew they'd walk out of there and never return.

As he stepped down into the family room, he picked up the remote and turned the TV back on to the breaking news. Crews were now outside Iris O'Connell's house, and the cameras were going crazy as the family pulled up. Each of them walked in the house and closed the door.

So a body that should never have been found had been dug up by a dog. The soil, evidently, had eroded, and the DA was under the impression that the body was Raymond O'Connell's.

The problem was that Raymond O'Connell didn't exist.

Chapter Fifteen

"No, stay home," Marcus said to Charlotte over the phone. "Don't come over here, and if any reporters call or show up, don't talk to them. I love you."

He hung up and pulled at his tie, loosening it, because it was beginning to choke him. He stood in his mom's kitchen, which was now put back together, listening to the shower running, knowing his mom was taking a well-deserved long one. His siblings were in the living room with Jack, talking about the situation they were all in.

"So how's everything at home?" Luke said, striding into the kitchen, where Marcus had gone to make a quick call, thinking he'd be talking to Alison, not Charlotte.

"Well, Charlotte's home," he said. "Seems that asshole Lonnie decided she had a conflict of interest and basically told her to go home and not come back. He fired her." Marcus was livid, wanting to wrap his hands around the man's neck.

Where had Harold been? Not there, evidently. He'd been assigned the shit job of giving out speeding tickets at a spot just outside town. Well, at least Charlotte wouldn't be in the lion's den, so to speak. Small blessings. He wouldn't share that thought with her.

"You knew that was coming, though, didn't you?" Luke said. He pulled open the fridge, reached for two beers, and held one out for Marcus, who just shook his head. Luke rested it on the island before unscrewing the top of his and taking a swallow. "I think we should talk about what's next, here. Jack was just saying the evidence in the case, although circumstantial, could tie it up. The blood match on Dad's letter is key. Man, would I love to get my hands on that letter…" He lifted the beer and took another swallow. "Why do you think she kept it?"

Marcus didn't want to rehash that big why. He'd wondered the same thing. Then there was the body and the fact that he and his siblings knew about the blood at the house, and the knife. That was the one thing the DA didn't have: the knife. He just shook his head.

"I don't know," Marcus said, unsure what he was supposed to feel. "Maybe we should be asking who the body is. There's been no ID, but is it Dad? I can't help wondering if it is."

For a split second, he saw something out back. He wasn't sure, but it was likely a reporter thinking he could sneak about and get some photos of the family in a private moment to splash across the papers, the internet, for the world to see.

"Ah, fuck…" He started to the back door.

"What?" Luke asked.

"Reporter, I think, sneaking around back, by the shed. Thought I saw him back there." He pulled open the door and stepped outside, then strode across the yard, still hearing voices from the front of the house. Their privacy was gone.

As he really dug into each step, he could feel his fury,

his anger, which had been pent up from this shitshow, coming to a boiling point. He'd somehow kept it under wraps until now. He knew Luke was right behind him as he rounded the corner of the shed, but he saw nothing.

Luke looked over the back fence and the alley it led out to, then pulled open the back gate and stepped out ahead of him, but there was no one there, nothing other than fences and garbage cans.

"No one," Luke said, looking around. He walked over to the neighbor's fence and looked over.

Marcus took a second, knowing he'd seen something. This was the type of cat and mouse shit he hated. "You know, I hate to say this, Luke, but I think it would be best if Mom didn't stay here…"

Then he heard a footstep, and he whipped around to see a man, his height, older, with gray hair—and something about him was familiar. He wore a black T-shirt and blue jeans with a jacket overtop.

"Marcus…" the man said.

He didn't know why, but he felt as if the air had left his lungs.

"Luke," the man added, looking over to his brother, who he knew was right beside him. "You both look good. Marcus, you still have that mark on your neck that you were born with." The man gestured to the odd-shaped mole just under his chin. His blue eyes were so much like his, and maybe it was because he was so damn tired, but Marcus's brain was short-circuiting. He glanced over to Luke, who didn't pull his gaze from the man. Who the hell was this?

"So you aren't dead, after all. I knew it," Luke said, sounding so pissed. He shook his head.

The man gave everything to him before looking over to

Marcus. "I met your niece, Alison, and that little girl you adopted, Eva."

What the fuck? was the only thing that kept going through his mind. "You met my daughter and Alison? Where? What the fuck is this, some kind of sick joke? Who are you?" He felt the pinch of his jaw as he ground out the words.

"Would say this is good old Dad," Luke said. "You look the same almost, older. Never forgot your face, even though I was so young. Isn't this just a kick in the ass? So what is this?" He really did sound pissed.

Marcus didn't think he'd heard right, but as he really looked at the man, he knew it was true.

"Your mother found herself in some trouble," Raymond said. "It was all over the news."

He took in the man's big hands, just like his, which he fisted by his sides, and his broad chest. He was a man who looked after himself, yet he had left his family. Like, holy shit! They needed to get him in the house, to call the DA, to get these damn charges dropped in this bullshit case.

"She's being charged with murder, your murder," Luke said. "Yet here you stand, Raymond O'Connell, in the flesh. You walked out on your family like the coward you are, leaving your wife and six kids to figure it out. So where've you been all these years, Pops? Tried looking for you for a long time. You know what I found?"

"There is no Raymond O'Connell," the man said. He had a deep low voice, a little raspy and very direct.

Marcus had never felt his mouth so dry. He reminded himself to pull in a breath. Maybe Luke's questions had prompted him to go into cop mode, as he realized he couldn't take Raymond in the house.

"Yeah, I figured that out," Luke said. "But that just created a lot more questions. So why?"

Evidently, his brother was the only one of them who could think on his feet, because Marcus was trying to wrap his head around who this man was. Never in a million years…

"I don't understand," Marcus said. "If you're here, who was wrapped in that tarp in that grave in the woods? Then there's the letter you left Mom. Evidently, it had blood on it. The night you left, she said you were acting strangely. Something happened, and she found your downstairs office wrecked, covered with blood, and a knife. You know she had Owen bury it? But someone saw him, and here we are. From what I'm thinking, this is a mess you created, a mess you're responsible for, and we're caught in the fallout."

He said nothing for a second, giving Marcus everything, before he reached into his coat and pulled out an envelope. He held it out to him.

"What is this?" he said but didn't take it.

It was Luke who reached over, took the envelope, and opened it. Marcus couldn't look away from the man. His brain was starting to put two and two together, and he remembered his father in the kitchen, making pancakes.

"It will clear your mother," Raymond said. "I can at least do that much before I leave."

Leave? Like, what the hell?

"It's handwritten," Luke said, but Marcus only glanced at it.

"It's the same handwriting as the letter in the evidence they're using against your mother," Raymond said. "It's a confession from me, saying I heard about the news, and the man in question was someone I worked with, did business with. He won't be in the system because he doesn't exist, either. His identity will be sealed because of national security or something. I already emailed a copy to the DA an hour ago and to the Feds in case he tries to bury it. They can test the handwriting, but it'll match."

Marcus wasn't sure what to make of Luke's expression as he read the letter. Was it confusion? Luke lifted the letter in the air, tapping it with his finger, still pissed off. Good.

"Yeah, it's all here," he said. "There are details of what happened, how he stabbed the man, one Sergey Ivanov, over a disagreement. He was afraid for his family and left a letter but didn't realize the man's blood was on it. He buried the body, and he outlines the details of where, exactly, at the edge of the state park, on Lionel's property, in a blue tarp. He says the man had a passion for cigars and was missing the first digit of his pinkie finger on his right hand, and there would've been a gold gentleman's ring with a ruby in the grave with him."

Marcus glanced over to Raymond. He had to remind himself what he'd said, that Raymond O'Connell didn't exist. So who were Marcus and his siblings, then?

"If I'm correct, that's evidence the DA won't have disclosed, but it will give credibility, and the case against your mother will be dismissed," Raymond said.

Luke said nothing. Marcus found himself glancing over to his mom's house before looking back at the man.

"So whose body was it, really?" Luke asked.

"Does it matter?"

"I suppose not," Luke said. "Toss them a Russian name and some details and make it go away. I guess that's all we could hope for."

The man kicked at a rock and then glanced around. Marcus knew he was about to leave, but he had a million questions, and not one of them mattered.

"So who are you, really, if you're not Raymond O'Connell? You said he doesn't exist. What was this, here, with Mom? You married her, had six kids, and then just disappeared one night?"

The man gave him everything, and there was something in his expression, in his eyes, that made Marcus wonder for a moment whether he could feel any remorse. "Found myself caught up in a fantasy," he said. "For a time, I thought I could have it. I was playing at something that seemed real enough. Thought I could walk away from the life that had been picked for me, but it caught up with me." Then the man looked over to the house, and he wondered if he had fond memories at all of them, of this place.

"Your mom looks good," Raymond said. "Karen looks just like her, and Suzanne looks like my mother. Owen, Ryan… Well, it would've been nice to catch up." He stopped talking.

"So what happened downstairs that night, really?" Marcus said. "Mom said you were acting strangely, and suddenly there were people coming over that she didn't know."

Luke hadn't pulled his gaze from Raymond. He had his arms crossed over his chest, studying him.

The man seemed to consider something, then made an odd sound and shook his head. "So that's what she said," he replied. He didn't smile, but he did take a step back. "You can't hide forever. I'd hoped to, but then…" The man who was his father gestured toward them. "I've got to go. That letter is your mom's get-out-of-jail-free card—but do me a favor. Don't tell her where you got it."

He went to turn, to walk away, and Marcus wanted to call him back, but Luke slapped a hand over his chest, maybe to stop him from taking a step.

"Why did you kill him?" Marcus called out. He just couldn't stop himself from asking.

The man turned back to him with a confused look. "Who?" he asked.

"The man in the woods, the one you buried," Marcus said.

All the man did was shake his head. "Who said I did?"

Then the person he could think of only as Raymond O'Connell walked away, shoving his hands in his pockets.

Marcus dragged his gaze over to Luke, who still had his hand on his chest, watching their father walk away.

"Let's go," Luke said, then somehow had him turned back and in the yard. He closed the gate.

"Did that just happen?" Marcus said, gesturing over the gate with his thumb. They started back to the house, Marcus still trying to wrap his head around this entire nightmare.

"Yeah," Luke said. "Seems good old Dad showed up to save the day."

As he pulled open the back door to step inside, he could hear his family's voices, and he took in his mom, who was crying, wearing a bathrobe, her hair wrapped in a towel. Suzanne was hugging her. Ryan and Jenny appeared shell-shocked, and Jack was dragging his hand over his face, his cell phone to his ear.

"Yes, thank you," Jack said, then hung up and took them all in. "Well, I don't know how to explain this, any of this, but that was Eileen, at the DA's office. Seems some evidence turned up, a confession from Raymond O'Connell, that basically exonerates you, Iris. I don't know what kind of guardian angel you have watching over you, but…" He was shaking his head.

Marcus took in his family. Karen was beside Jack, and Owen was leaning on the island, Tessa's hands on his shoulders.

"So Raymond O'Connell, our father, just confessed to

a murder and sent a letter to the DA? What the hell does this mean?" Owen said.

Marcus could hear what wasn't being said, the questions that would likely be asked over the next few days, but as he pulled in a breath to explain, his mom dried her eyes and stood up, lifting her hands in the air as if to tell them she was okay.

"It means this bullshit case against Mom goes away," Luke said. "That's what this means, and nothing else really matters, does it?" He tossed Marcus a glance.

"Luke's right," Marcus finally said. "Mom's cleared, and this goes away. That's all that matters."

Luke slipped into the living room alone and walked over to the window, pulling back the curtains, seeing the media circus still outside. He wondered if one day he'd believe what he'd said.

"So how long do you think they'll be out there?" Marcus said as he followed his brother into the living room.

"Oh, I'd say until they find someone else's life to rip apart," Luke replied, then slapped a hand over Marcus's shoulder. "You should go home to your wife and that little girl. Give them a kiss from me."

"What about them?" Marcus said, tilting his head toward their siblings. "Don't you think they have a right to know about Dad, him being here, what happened? Then there's Mom. Don't you think she'll ask?"

He wasn't sure what to make of the expression on Luke's face. He seemed to consider it, then shook his head. "Maybe one day we'll tell them, but did you see Mom's face in there? Because I did. That woman said her good-byes to our father a long time ago. Let sleeping dogs lie, big brother. Go on home to your wife."

Marcus didn't know why, but there was just something

about today, about all this, that told him Luke was right. He just wanted time with his wife and his little girl. So he started to the door, then put his hand on the knob, glancing back to Luke. "You knew all along that Dad wasn't who we thought he was?"

Luke said nothing for a second. Then an odd smile touched his lips. "It's the world I work in. Give my best to Charlotte."

So Marcus stepped out of the house, taking in the cameras, the media circus, the reporters. He started the two-block walk to his home, and he realized that unsettled feeling he'd been carrying for so long had finally disappeared.

Undone

Get your facts first, then you can distort them as
you please.

Mark Twain

Chapter Sixteen

The morning after a big case, Jack felt a moment of peace. This was unlike his usual mornings, when his mind immediately kicked in with everything he needed to accomplish, forcing him out of bed before he could enjoy a moment with his wife.

The sun was just coming up, and the breeze fluttered the curtains of the open window. He ran his hands over the flat of Karen's silky-smooth stomach. Her butt was nestled against him, and he traced the outline of her breasts, feeling the handful and enjoying the soft whisper she made as he stirred her from sleep. He pressed a kiss to her shoulder, her neck, touching her, loving the feel of her against him. He maneuvered her, still half asleep, over onto her back.

God damn, she was beautiful.

He ran his hand over her leg, her thigh, just imagining himself inside her again as he pressed a kiss to her lips. He took in her image, the way her eyes fluttered open and her hands linked over his shoulders, pulling him to her. She ran her hands over his back, feeling him, touching him in the way she did that drove him over the edge. He was so ready for her, to settle inside her again as he had the night before, feeling her come apart around him—but he couldn't shake this need for something more.

"I want a baby, kids…" he said.

She froze and stiffened beneath him, then somehow pressed her hands to his chest and pushed him back. She slid from under him and sat up in bed, pulling at the sheet until it was up and over her breasts, leaving him with nothing. Her expression wasn't even the least bit amused.

She brushed her hand over her hair, pushing it back, now wide awake. "Did you just say you wanted kids, a baby, with me?"

He was lying on his side, naked and cooling off, the mood gone. He hung his head for a second, because she didn't have to say anything else for him to know she wasn't on the same page.

"Yes," he said. "It's time, Karen. I want to build our family. I want kids—and seriously, who else would I have kids with?" He went to pull the sheet from her, but she was shaking her head as she scooted back away from him to the other side of the bed.

"And you just…what, suddenly want to get me pregnant? Right, I guess I should have figured that out last night, but in my haste, as I felt the weight of everything my mom's been through being lifted from me, I kind of got lost in the moment with you. I love you, Jack, but I'm not ready for kids. I love working, being a lawyer, being selfish, and…" She stopped talking and pulled her lower lip between her teeth.

He could see how much she was thinking—no, overthinking. So he climbed from bed and walked naked around it to the en suite, then stepped into the walk-in shower and turned it on. He let the hot spray settle over him as he pressed his hands to the shower wall and just let the water run down his back. When he felt a hand there, he glanced over his shoulder and took in Karen, who had joined him.

"So is that how we have a conversation?" she said. "You get up and leave?"

He just stared for a second, at a loss of what to say. "What conversation? I said I wanted kids, a baby, and you said no. I think the conversation is over."

She reached for a bar of soap. He could hear the phone ringing in the background, but he wasn't too inclined to race out of the shower for it. His wife soaped her hands and ran them over his chest. He loved the feel of her touch, and something in her blue eyes seemed to hint at mischief.

"No, the conversation's not over," she said. "And that's not what I said. You have to give me a second, Jack, to get my head around this and discuss it. You know, the talking thing."

Right, that thing she did when she talked and talked about something and he heard only half of it. She could cut out two thirds of what she was saying and get to the point and save an incredible amount of time.

"So you want to discuss having children? Is that what you're saying?" He let out a laugh that bordered on frustration as she touched him teasingly, and he leaned his head back and shut his eyes.

"I want to hear why you want them and why you suddenly feel the need to have them now." She was debating this.

"You want me to give you an argument, as in the reasons why we should have kids now? Oh, I don't know. I'm ready, we're not getting younger, and…"

"So now I'm getting too old?" She pulled her hands

back, and for a second, he wondered whether he was walking into a trap.

"No, Karen, you're not too old, but we're not twenty anymore. We have a law practice now, so why does having a baby mean you can't be a lawyer? Take a little time off after the baby, but you can still work. I'm not expecting you to be and do everything." He took the soap from her and started running it over her body, without a clue what she was thinking.

"So you wouldn't expect me to suddenly stay home and take up baking and cooking and raising your kids?"

"Good God, no."

She turned around, and he took in the mischief in her blue eyes.

He shrugged. "You can't cook, anyway."

She made a face and poked him.

He heard knocking at the door, and then the phone started ringing again.

"Someone is persistent," he said, then rinsed off and stepped out of the shower, grabbing a towel and running it over his hair and body quickly before wrapping it around his waist. He heard the knocking again.

He could hear Karen still in the shower as the phone went silent, and he strode to the door and pulled it open.

In the hall, Luke was dressed casually in blue jeans and a deep blue T-shirt with a hoodie overtop, his shades nestled into his short, wavy dark hair. "Took you long enough," he said, letting his gaze travel down to the towel. He strode in without being asked. "Sorry to drag you from your shower."

Jack gave the door a shove closed. "So was that you calling, as well, or is someone else needing to get a hold of me?"

"Oh, no, that was me. You got coffee on yet?" Luke

made his way into the kitchen and over to Karen's fancy espresso machine.

"No, but make me one over there, since you've made yourself at home already."

He was still getting used to Karen's family showing up, and he still had trouble with their need to be so involved in one another's lives.

"So who's here…?" Karen said as she stepped out of the bedroom, a towel around her hair and her robe pulled on. She stepped over to Jack, sliding her arm around his waist, settling her hand on his towel, which lingered there. "Luke, hey. What's going on?"

Jack took her in as they waited for Luke to say something. He went to make an espresso but seemed to be having trouble.

"Get out of my kitchen," Karen said, taking over. "You're going to wreck my machine." She filled it with fresh coffee and tamped it down, and Luke moved away and let his gaze settle on Jack.

"I called the phone company this morning and changed Mom's phone number," he said. "It's unlisted now. She got a number of calls last night—threatening ones, you know, calling her a murderer and saying everyone always knew she'd done something, that she should be strapped to a stake and burned alive and she'd better pack up and leave town if she knows what's good for her."

Karen's expression said everything. "I knew it would be bad, but really…?" She gestured vaguely, at a loss, but Jack knew the depth of emotion some people operated from, and he shook his head.

"Good," he said. "At least that will stop the calls."

Luke lifted his hand, gesturing to the TV. "You watch the news this morning?"

"No, I was sleeping. Why would I?"

Luke walked over to the TV and turned it on. "Oh, just because the news is having a heyday with this whole thing." He was flicking through channels and then landed on one of the local stations, with a byline running underneath: *Charges dropped in murder case against Iris O'Connell.*

"So…" Jack started.

The image flashed to the DA, Tibo Lewis, and beside him was Lonnie, with an "Acting Sheriff" byline under his name. Evidently, a press conference had been called. Jack just stared at the screen.

"Good morning, everyone," Tibo said. "In light of recent evidence that was just brought to the attention of the DA's office last night, the state will not be pursuing charges against Iris O'Connell and has dropped all charges against her. Although we can't comment on the investigation regarding the remains that were discovered, as it is still ongoing, the evidence that was provided has exonerated Mrs. O'Connell."

Jack took in Karen, who walked over to him. He could hear the reporters calling out questions, but of course, Tibo was leaving them hanging.

Tibo gestured to Lonnie and said, "I understand you all have questions regarding the O'Connells, but right now, I would ask that you respect their privacy. As the investigation is ongoing, I will turn this over to the acting sheriff, who will be able to answer some questions."

Jack crossed his arms over his chest, taking in the TV.

Luke glanced back and then gestured to the press conference. "Oh, just you wait. It gets better."

Jack wasn't sure what he meant. He took in the deputy he knew Marcus had problems with, definitely no one he'd have picked for sheriff. There was just something about him he'd never liked.

"Yes, Doreen." Lonnie gestured to one of the reporters.

"If the murder charge has been dropped against Iris O'Connell, can you tell us if any of the O'Connell children will be implicated in the murder of Raymond O'Connell? Will Marcus O'Connell be reinstated as sheriff anytime soon?"

Jack thought his eyes bugged out, and he heard Karen hiss beside him.

"I can't comment on an ongoing investigation or any suspects we are considering. As far as Marcus O'Connell is concerned, he is currently on leave pending an investigation into his misconduct and breach of authority in the handling of this investigation. Remember, folks, Marcus was not elected to the position of sheriff but only fell into it when Sheriff Osbert Berry unexpectedly retired."

"What an asshole," Karen said rather calmly.

The news flashed back to the anchors, who brought up an image of the family walking out of the courtroom the day before. "The DA's decision today to drop all charges in this case, in my experience, bothers me," said one of the anchors. "Here's a replay of the family leaving the courthouse yesterday. If you look at their body language, the emotionless stare is quite unusual and only confirms that the family is aware of who killed Raymond O'Connell. Maybe the wrong family member was charged in the murder, but looking at this family, who also appear arrogant and unremorseful—"

Jack ripped the remote from Luke's hand and turned off the TV, then tossed the remote down on the counter. "So the court of opinion is working overtime. Please, for everyone's sake, keep the news off. Look, you know how this works. We'll go out tonight, everyone, to a restaurant, all of us. Let the town get a look at us, get the gossip and stuff out of their system. As far as Lonnie, we know he has an ax to grind with Marcus. I'll have to call Marcus and Tibo, because after that little stunt, Lonnie may have just screwed any chance of your brother being re-elected."

Karen looked pissed, and Luke gave him a steely, hard stare that he'd never want to cross.

"You don't think that was the plan all along?" Karen asked.

Jack took in his wife and her brother, who already knew the truth. Karen was no longer relaxed, and baby talk was now far off the table. What was he supposed to say?

"What bothers me more than anything," Luke said, cutting in, "is that he alluded to the body being that of Raymond O'Connell, dear old Dad, considering we all know that's not true."

"I'll call the DA, go and meet with him about that stunt," Jack said. "Unfortunately, without Raymond O'Connell coming forward in person to shut this down, the rumors will continue and will likely get worse. We need to remember that even though the charges were dropped, doubts will remain in the minds of everyone in the community, telling them that the O'Connells did something."

Chapter Seventeen

"Good morning, sunshine. You sleep okay?" Ryan said as he poured himself another cup of coffee, dressed in blue jeans and an old T-shirt, barefoot, because he was taking today off, as well.

Alison said nothing and gave him nothing, just walked around him and waited for him to move so she could pour herself a mug of coffee. She dumped in what seemed to him like a ton of sugar and stirred it with a spoon.

"You know it would probably do your grandma some good if you went and hung out with her today," he added.

Alison shrugged.

He and Jenny had told her the night before that she'd be staying home from school for the next little bit, considering the spotlight. It seemed time was all that would settle the talk in town.

At the same time, he could see from her lack of response that something was up, so he leaned on the counter, closer to her, to wait her out. Unfortunately, she was really good at going dark and silent.

"So how's Brady? You talk to him lately?" he said. Maybe the boy would be the thing to loosen her tongue.

She held the mug and stared down into the coffee. "Saw him yesterday. Went and hung out at his place for a bit. But I got a text this morning. His dad said they're leaving."

Oh, so that was it. Boy trouble with a boy who was leaving town. Good! But Ryan had to remind himself that he'd have felt that way about any boy right about now. "Well, that's too bad. So where are they going? Didn't you tell me they just moved here? That's kind of sudden, isn't it?"

His daughter rested her mug on the island, and he took in her messy hair , the makeup she'd slept in, and the nightshirt that stopped at midthigh.

"Yeah, he moved here right before the Jackson Moore thing happened at school," she said. "He was nice. When I was over there yesterday, he said nothing about leaving. It was weird, you know, the way his dad kept watching us. He wouldn't leave us alone—kind of like how you acted, Dad." She wasn't teasing. In fact, she sounded accusatory and mad, and she made a face. "Figured maybe you talked to him or something."

"Hate to break this to you, Alison, but I didn't have the pleasure of meeting Brady's dad, so I couldn't have talked to him. But I'll remember that for the future," he teased, though he knew she wasn't impressed. At least now he wouldn't have to figure out a way to get a background check done on Brady and his father.

Alison glanced up to him, her brows furrowed. "But he said he knew you," she said.

That had him really looking at her, and he shook his head. "What's his dad's name? I don't remember meeting anyone who recently moved here. How did he know me?"

She just shrugged. "I don't know. He just said he did. Kind of thought he knew Uncle Marcus, too."

Maybe he should've asked Brady who his dad was. If he knew him, he'd have a better idea of what this was about. "So, for curiosity's sake, who is his dad, and where do they live, exactly?"

Alison took a swallow of coffee, and he thought she made a face, likely from all the sugar she dumped in there. "He lives a block away, closer to Grandma's. He said his name's Ray. When we first met him, I was in the park with Eva, and Brady was there, and his dad came looking for him and called him over. He found out that you're my dad and Eva is Uncle Marcus's daughter. I know they had just moved here and everything, but he really was kind of weird about staying close to home with Brady."

He had no idea who this Ray was.

Just then, he heard a knock at the locked front door, and he strode out of the kitchen to see his brother Marcus on the porch, dressed in blue jeans and a navy sweatshirt. Evidently, his return to the sheriff's office still hadn't happened, but then, it wouldn't be that easy. Ryan flicked the lock and pulled the door open.

"You see the news?" was all Marcus said.

Ryan didn't have to ask if it was bad news, considering his brother's tone. He heard the footsteps on the stairs and took in Jenny, showered and dressed in a pair of jeans and a T-shirt, her hair still damp.

"What's going on?" she said, evidently having heard.

Ryan found himself glancing out the door, wondering if reporters would show up next.

"That asshole Lonnie basically buried me on TV," Marcus said. "Other than that, the DA announced he'd dropped the charges, but the kicker is that they're still implying the remains are dear old Dad's, and we could still find ourselves under investigation, charged, and arrested. You know, in other words, they're shining the spotlight deep on all of us."

There was another knock at the door from behind them, and Ryan turned and spotted a deputy's uniform through the window. He pulled it open to find Harold standing there. For a second, he didn't know what to say.

Harold gestured with his thumb over to Marcus's place, across the street. "Charlotte said Marcus was over here."

Ryan pulled the door open without inviting him to come in. Maybe he was still remembering how Harold had cuffed his mother and stuffed her in the back of his cop car. Even though he'd tried to explain it was better him than Lonnie, the fact was that he'd still done it.

"Harold, there's coffee on," Jenny said. "Can I get you some?"

For a second, as he took her in, Ryan wondered why she'd done that.

Harold just shook his head. "I just wanted to stop in this morning because I'm not comfortable with how this has all gone down. Suzanne didn't come home last night…"

He heard the squeak and looked up to see his sister at the top of the stairs. She'd stayed over in their spare room at Jenny's insistence. She looked miserable, her hair a tangled mess, and she was wearing a pair of Jenny's pajama pants and an old T-shirt. She strode down, and Marcus rested his hand on the post, taking in Suzanne and Harold. No one said anything at first.

"So this is how we're doing things now," Harold said. "Or is this your way of saying it's over?"

Suzanne stopped at the bottom step, and Jenny slid her hand around Ryan's arm, pulling at him. "Maybe we should give these two a minute to talk alone," she said.

Suzanne was shaking her head. "No, we're good. There's nothing I have to say that my family can't hear. I think you said loud and clear that it was over when you arrested my mom. How could you do that to her? And don't say that it was your job, that it wasn't personal, because it was personal. You chose a side."

"Suzanne," Marcus cut in, sounding unusually calm. He slid his gaze to Harold, and Ryan could see there was an edge there, that he was struggling with the same feeling of betrayal. "That's not the way of it. Harold's hands were tied. He basically had no choice—and he was right: If Lonnie had picked up Mom, it would've been worse for her."

"What you did wasn't right," Suzanne said, then stepped off the last step and started into the kitchen.

Harold hesitated a second. "Excuse me," he said, turning to Ryan and Jenny and gesturing toward her. "Do you mind?"

Jenny nodded, and Harold followed Suzanne into the kitchen, where Alison was. She'd get a front-row seat to the show.

"So are we going to let them…?"

"Work it out?" Jenny said. "Yes, if that's what you mean."

Marcus was still standing there, looking past him to the kitchen. He settled his hand on the door. "Yeah, I hate to admit it, but Jenny's right. They're either going to work it out or not. Besides, I've got to go and figure out how to rein in Lonnie, who's doing his very best to make sure he kills any chance I have of getting my job back, let alone getting re-elected. God damn! Sometimes I really hate politics, but it seems Lonnie has found his calling. If only the people out there had any idea of the real man behind the face…" His cell phone rang, and he pulled it out. "And it begins," he said. "The mayor."

As Marcus answered the phone and stepped out of the house, Ryan took in Jenny. They listened to the back and forth between Suzanne and Harold, but for some reason, Ryan was still stuck on that boy, Brady, who was leaving.

His dad knew him? He wasn't sure why, but something about that bothered him.

"So do we intrude, or…?" Ryan finally said.

"We head over to your mom's," Jenny replied. "I'm kind of worried about her. Thought we could check on her, maybe do some errands for her, or maybe just get her out of the house, you know?"

"And what about Harold and Suzanne? Do we just leave them?" He could hear their discussion, which was far from quiet—but that was Suzanne. She didn't take anything lying down.

Jenny went up on her tiptoes, slid her arms around his shoulders, and settled against him. "Yeah, that's exactly what we do. So go get dressed. I'll drag Alison from the kitchen, and then maybe Harold and Suzanne will have some time to work things out. In case you didn't know, she loves him, and he loves her. The biggest problem here is that he still had a job to do, and in case you all didn't notice, he went out of his way to make sure your mom didn't get screwed. He stayed on the job for your mom, for Marcus, because of what was coming down. If he hadn't been there, I'd hate to think how much worse it would have been."

Then she kissed him and strode into the kitchen, and he just stared at the woman he was madly, deeply in love with, wondering how she could see something that he couldn't.

Chapter Eighteen

Marcus pulled up in front of City Hall and parked just as his cell phone rang again, Jack's name on the screen.

"Hi, Jack," he said, making a point of not looking at anyone, because there were just too many people around. Whereas before they would've offered a friendly hello, now they had turned nasty and angry, with hateful stares. Then there were the whispers, as if they didn't think he could hear.

"Where are you right now?" Jack said. "Because I called Charlotte, and she said you left, that you had some things to take care of. I seriously hope that doesn't mean Lonnie. Just in case you're wondering, Luke stopped by, and we saw the news. You're not doing something stupid, are you?"

He didn't know why he smiled at the sound of his brother-in-law's voice. Jack was suddenly a pit bull for their family and was basically there to save their asses. He'd never have imagined Jack was the one who'd come through for them.

"Like, what, killing Lonnie, you mean?" Marcus said as he got out and began walking. There was silence on the other end for a second.

"Don't you dare joke about something like that," Jack said. "You are joking, right?"

He wished he could see Jack's expression. At times, the man could be so uptight and serious. "Yeah, relax. Even though I want to wrap my hands around his throat, I won't. I did get a call, though, from the mayor. Evidently, I've been summoned before the city council, so this should be interesting. They're likely going to ask me all kinds of questions, including whether I killed my dad. Oh, yeah, did you miss on the news how they never mentioned that Raymond O'Connell was the one who reached out to clear our mom, so the body in the woods couldn't have been his? He basically confessed to killing the man, and he tossed out a name, too. That was a pretty major omission on the part of the DA and Lonnie. It seems they still want the spotlight to shine our way. They left enough threads hanging to make sure the public still sees us O'Connells as guilty. But, hey, if you can't have one O'Connell, doesn't matter. You can still get another. Just as long as you destroy all their lives, right?" He knew he sounded like an asshole.

Jack sighed. "Okay, so we're in that headspace, are we?" he said. "Don't think I don't get it. I do, completely, but having a pity party isn't going to solve anything. Besides, I'm here now, about to go in and see the DA, so since you're already here, meet me in the DA's office. This involves you and that stunt they pulled this morning. The mayor and council can wait."

Then Jack hung up, and Marcus just held his cell phone, staring at it. He'd never expected to actually follow an order from Jack. He really was taking his role too seriously. At the same time, he hated to admit it, but having

Jack all over this mess, helping to sort it out, allowed him to breathe easier.

Being without his badge, his duty belt, and his gun as he walked into a building he'd been inside so many times, he couldn't help feeling as if everything he was had been taken from him.

Marcus strode up the steps to where the DA's office was, seeing reporters here and there, and a camera flashed in his face.

"Marcus, can you give us a statement as to why the DA dropped the charges against your mother and what your involvement was? And can you explain why you, as sheriff, looked the other way when an allegation of a crime was made because it concerned your family? Can you see why that was a problem? Did you destroy and hide evidence?"

"Marcus, over here!" Jack called out, likely because Marcus was about to rip the camera from the asshole reporter and tell him to go fuck himself.

Right, he was supposed to be holding himself in check, except it didn't seem to matter what he did, because they'd make something up anyway. A hand touched his arm, and he realized Jack would likely drag him away if he had to.

"Hey, no questions," Jack said, pulling him away, toward the office of Eileen, the assistant DA. "The sheriff isn't answering anything."

Inside the office, Eileen was dressed in a black pantsuit, and Tibo in a navy suit. Jack shut the door behind them, and Marcus pulled off his shades, which he'd deliberately left on until then, and rested them on top of his head.

"So that was quite the stunt this morning," Marcus said. "You dropped the charges but didn't clear up the questions about whether my mother and my family are involved, or whether the body is Raymond O'Connell's."

The expression on Tibo's face was smug, that asshole.

Marcus hadn't realized until now that this was like a game to him.

"Conclusively, we haven't been able to disprove that it's—"

"That's bullshit and you know it, Tibo," Jack cut in. "Considering the Feds were given the same evidence, a copy of the letter, I'm thinking maybe it's time to bring them in, let them take over, and launch an investigation into the DA's office on its handling of this case. You manufactured evidence against Iris O'Connell and then Marcus, having him removed as sheriff, all because he openly called out one of the district judges, a judge you've supported, for his blatant bias. How long, you think, before people start to see this as payback for Marcus not looking the other way?

"And let's not forget that the handwriting on the confession letter matches that from the letter taken into evidence from Iris O'Connell's house. That search wasn't justified, but then, isn't it funny that it was Judge Root who signed off on the warrant, the same judge Marcus was coming after? I think the Feds will be taking a pretty hard look at that, don't you? Don't you think the people of Livingston would like to know how the DA managed to get a warrant without the kind of evidence and probable cause needed, an open warrant for a fishing expedition on a case with no direct evidence tied to Iris O'Connell?

"And what did you uncover, anyway? Some belongings Iris kept to remember her husband—who, by the way, left her with nothing more than a note that said not to look for him. You questioned her integrity and asked why she wouldn't call the police to report a man missing after he walked out and left her a Dear Jane letter? This whole case was a witch hunt from the beginning, based on hearsay, no evidence. Just so there's no misunderstanding, we will be seeking damages and restitution.

Then there's the sheriff. You overstepped in having Marcus removed, and that press conference with Lonnie to further destroy his credibility was pure slander. You know it. Do you want to tie this office up in another lawsuit?"

Eileen was shaking her head, and Marcus could see she wasn't on the same page as the DA. At the same time, she said nothing, which wasn't like her. Maybe she'd been slapped down again by Tibo, but at what point would she step up and take a stand?

"Right," Tibo said. "You want to talk about that letter we found tucked away in the basement? It didn't just say goodbye and not to look for him. Your mother may not have killed Raymond O'Connell, but she isn't completely innocent. I wonder how the O'Connell children would feel if they knew what was really in that letter."

Marcus didn't know what to say to that. Jack glanced to him, and he felt the warning there as something in his stomach knotted and that sick feeling he'd had when this all began returned.

"Where's the letter?" Jack demanded. "We want it returned. I'm done with this game of yours, these insinuations you're making to try to destroy this family's credibility."

"You sure you want the letter back?" Tibo said.

Marcus knew the DA was playing him, and he could almost hear Jack warning him not to take the bait.

Jack laughed under his breath, the kind of laugh that meant Tibo was pushing in a way that could bite him. "Yes," he said, "and let me be clear: If any of the contents are leaked to the press or used in any way to intimidate my client or her family, you'll have a problem, more of a problem than you do now, considering that stunt you and Lonnie pulled this morning."

"I never told Lonnie to say what he did," Tibo said. "The charges against your mom were dropped…"

"Not good enough, Tibo," Jack said, cutting him off. "Either you issue a direct and very clear statement that the remains are not those of Raymond O'Connell and you completely, publicly exonerate my clients, meaning Iris O'Connell and all the O'Connell siblings, or I will bring down on this office the kind of lawsuit that could bankrupt this county, and we'll fight it out in the news. I'll pull out every skeleton this office has hidden, the cases it hasn't prosecuted, the preferential treatment you've shown, the deals you've given to one class of people while running roughshod over others. I will show easily that this office has continued to wield systematic racism and classism against the people, and the fact is that this all started because the sheriff wasn't willing to let anyone walk because of who they were.

"I'll even go so far as to bring up how the DA's office has overlooked the unfair sentencing practices of Judge Root, the discrimination, the rights violations. Then there's the prosecutorial misconduct. We can go back years if you want. I will turn this into a living nightmare for you and bring all of this to your doorstep, Tibo, and you know what will happen when I turn this into a media circus? You won't be able to shut it down. The people will be demanding your resignation, especially when they find out how they're on the hook, tax wise, for the county bill after your mishandling of this case, which I will win. The cost will have to be paid by the very people you're supposed to be protecting."

"What do you want?" Tibo said.

Eileen was hiding a smile, Marcus thought, by the way she lifted her hand and pulled it over her face. He crossed his arms, because he rather liked this pit-bull side of Jack.

He found himself leaning back against the desk, taking in the show.

"Well, one, by end of day, Marcus had better be re-appointed as sheriff, with a public apology that clears up any misconceptions that he did anything wrong—and you know what I'm talking about, Tibo. You'd better clear from the minds of this community, with one hundred percent certainty, any illusions about Marcus being involved in any kind of misconduct."

"Well, there is the matter of the knife," Tibo started.

"What knife?" Jack snapped. "You had better produce this knife right now, because I'm tired of hearing about it." He took another step closer. "Be careful, because what you're doing is setting a very dangerous precedent that any suspect can fabricate a story with no evidence in order to get a deal. You damn well know that Marcus has been fairer to the people here than any sheriff. He hasn't been a crook or anything like that. I'm pretty sure you've already had a call this morning from Senator Edwards, telling you to clean up this mess."

Tibo made a face as if considering, and his eye twitched ever so slightly. Jack really was good. This was the first Marcus was hearing about the senator, and he couldn't pull his gaze from Jack.

"I'll make the statement," Tibo said, then glanced over to Marcus. "But whether Marcus is reinstated is up to the mayor and the council, who, as I understand it, are expecting him to answer some questions this morning."

Jack stepped back. "I think we're done here," he said. "Let's go pay a visit to the mayor and council."

Marcus knew Jack was behind him, his hand on the door, ready to pull it open. He took in Eileen, who'd said nothing, then dragged his gaze back over to Tibo and took a step toward him. "Answer me this," he said. "How much of this was because I rocked the boat with Judge Root, because I stepped on toes I was told not to?"

"You don't think your actions have consequences?" Tibo said. He jutted his chin to Jack. "I'll call the press and make an announcement by noon."

Jack pulled open the door. "Marcus," was all he said.

Marcus knew he wouldn't get anything else, and he took in Jack, who was clearly waiting for him. So he took one step and then another out the door, Jack right behind him.

As they headed over to the stairs, he thought of Raymond O'Connell. His father was alive, and this entire nightmare was almost over, but the answers he had were ones he hadn't expected or wanted.

"So was that you who was responsible for the senator's call?" Marcus said as they stepped off the last stair and made their way to the mayor's office.

"Well, considering that press conference this morning didn't officially clear any of you, I knew the DA was going to need a little more persuasion."

"So what did that call cost you?" he said. He knew the life Jack had come from. Calling in that kind of favor always cost something.

Ahead of them were the glass doors to the mayor's office, but Marcus dragged his gaze over to Jack, who could've written the book on pulling off a poker face.

"A favor down the road," he said. "Nothing I can't live with to rescue my family from a witch hunt."

They stopped just outside the door, and Marcus took in the man his sister loved, whom he'd never really accepted into the family. He wondered when Jack had really become one of them.

"In case I didn't say it, Jack, thank you for having our backs—my back."

Jack glanced away in amusement, he thought. "That was hard for you to choke out, wasn't it?"

He didn't need to say anything else. Jack was married to his sister, yes, but he realized that he was also a brother to him. "You have no idea."

Jack laughed under his breath, and Marcus pulled open the door and stepped into the mayor's office.

He still had more questions to answer, more hurdles to jump through, before he could get a piece of his life back. And, as far as he was concerned, Lonnie was still someone he had to deal with.

Chapter Nineteen

"So where is Mom tonight?" Ryan asked, handing Jack a short glass of bourbon. Jack didn't drink often, but tonight was different.

"She opted to stay home," Luke said, holding a beer, from where he lounged on the sofa at Ryan and Jenny's place. "It's been pretty quiet since that news conference at noon. Still don't know how you managed to pull that off, but it had all the reporters packing up from outside Mom's house and leaving her alone."

Charlotte was sitting on the loveseat with Marcus, her bare feet up on his lap for him to massage. Her hand rested on her pregnant belly. His gun and badge were at his place, Jack knew, where he'd taken them off just an hour earlier.

"I'm not sure that's a good idea, Mom being alone…" Ryan started. He sat on the arm of Jenny's chair, and she rested her hand on his thigh and shook her head.

"Your mom needs some time alone after what she's been through," she said. "Come on, you guys. She just needs to find her footing again. I know how that feels. She's probably exhausted, with the stress of everything. Just give her some time and space. Besides, I think it's best we talk it out without your mom here to overhear. For one, how about that news conference this afternoon? I can't believe the DA got up and publicly apologized to Iris and all of us, saying they were contacted by Raymond O'Connell and the remains discovered have been confirmed not to be his, and the DA's office confirmed that the evidence in the case was circumstantial, with unfounded allegations manufactured to accuse Iris."

Jack lifted his glass, knowing that Tibo had followed exactly the outline he had given him. Senator Edwards had made it clear that the investigation of the remains was to be shut down and filed away under national security, because that was all he needed to say to put an end to any local investigation.

"You mean how he made himself look like the hero, as if he had personally investigated and made sure an innocent woman wasn't wrongly convicted?" Luke cut in. "Yeah, that was quite the show."

Jack pulled in a breath to speak, but there was a point, after all the talking, that he didn't want to talk anymore. He was exhausted from looking at the pitfalls and problems his family had created because of a secret that had been kept for too long.

"So what happened with the mayor, Marcus?" Owen said from where he sat in the window seat with Tessa beside him. Alison was upstairs with Eva, but they still kept their voices low. "I see you were reinstated as sheriff, but with this hunt for the knife that they were so dead set on finding, are you honestly saying they're dropping it?"

Karen was holding a glass of water, her second of the night, as she slid her hand around his shoulders and sat on his lap. He leaned back in the dining chair Marcus had dragged into the living room, letting his arm slide around her waist, his hand on her thigh. She wore a pink cotton sundress with a cream cardigan overtop.

Jack looked over to Marcus, knowing he likely didn't want to talk about it anymore.

"They had no choice but to give Marcus back the position," Harold said from where he stood, leaning against the post at the entry into the living room, with his arm around Suzanne. He was dressed down in blue jeans and a T-shirt, and everyone gave everything to him.

He was still working his way back into everyone's good graces, even though Jack was well aware that everything he'd done behind the scenes had been to protect this family, having found himself between a rock and a hard place.

"Harold is right," Jack said. "When Marcus and I arrived, you should all know that Harold had just finished calling the mayor and council on the carpet, advising them as to how Tibo had used an accusation from a suspect in another crime, and there was no evidence, and he had found nothing to warrant an investigation. As far as Lonnie is concerned, Harold told them he has a history of police overreach and misconduct, and Marcus has had to reprimand him many times for his mishandling of investigations. It was actually the former sheriff, Osbert Berry, who called the mayor personally this morning from where he's now retired, down in Arizona. He not only vouched for Marcus and his character but went to bat for him, calling out all the charges as bullshit."

Marcus pulled in a breath, appearing so tired. "It wasn't entirely that easy, Jack. You know the mayor and council had their minds made up, regardless of what anyone said, before we walked in there. I was done. You all should know that the mayor asked about the blood on the letter, the one in evidence, that matched the remains at the scene. Yes, apparently either Tibo or Lonnie shared all the details, which was totally not okay. Talk about misconduct... They also asked about the knife Owen buried, even though not even five minutes before that, Harold had been standing there, telling them there was no evidence that the knife burial had even happened. But you know that once a question is in people's mind, convincing them it's not true becomes downright impossible. Nevertheless, Jack left them no choice, not after that press conference from Tibo."

"I thought you mentioned that the mayor received a call while in that meeting," Karen said, cutting in and tapping his shoulder. It wasn't lost on him that she hadn't had one glass of wine that night.

Everyone was looking at him, because no one knew the contents of the call the mayor had received in the middle of their interrogation. Jack knew they'd never have agreed to reinstate Marcus otherwise, but that call had ended the meeting, and his badge had been returned. Jack knew well that the senator had made his position clear, first to Tibo and then to the mayor.

"So you called in a favor, did you, Jack?" Luke asked.

All Jack did was stare at the amber liquid in his glass, wondering when he'd be reminded to fall in line, when he'd get that call. Sooner, probably, than later. He figured next year, his family would start filling him in on plans to have him run for governor, then for senate. It was everything his family had expected of him, which he'd tried to turn away from, being part of a world where he'd be expected to give favors to a class of people who already ran the country and created the laws everyone else conformed to.

"No more than any of you would have done," he finally said.

No one said anything at first. Then Marcus cleared his

throat and took them all in. "Since we're talking, I think we need to come clean. No more secrets, right?"

Jack felt a tightness in his chest. From the glance between Marcus and Luke, it seemed that whatever he was going to tell them, Luke already knew.

"Am I going to want to hear this?" he said. Leaning against him, Karen stiffened and sat up, and her expression turned pissed. Suzanne turned to Harold, and from the way his mouth opened, Jack wasn't sure if the man was ready to hear anything else, either. Owen and Tessa, meanwhile, were relatively quiet again.

"Someone had better say something, because I've had enough secrets," Suzanne said.

"Yesterday, when you all received the news about how the charges were being dropped because the DA had received a letter from our dear old dad," Luke began, "Marcus and I were out back. Marcus had seen something, or someone. When we went into the alley, Dad was there."

Karen stood up, and he didn't think he'd ever forget her expression. "What? Dad... Why didn't you bring him inside? Are you sure?"

Everyone was talking now, and there it was: the ache, the pain, the hurt. He could hear it in each of them.

Marcus shook his head. "He gave Luke a copy of the letter to make sure Mom got off. He'd heard about it, and he came back to make it right..."

"Or he's been here all along," Luke cut in. "You should know that he said the body in the woods would never be identified, because he didn't exist, just like Dad. I suspected as much already from my own searching for him, but, as I told you all before, it's like he was a ghost. He had just disappeared, and then there he was again. Since Marcus is hell bent on everyone knowing, you should also know that whatever happened downstairs in the basement, even though Dad took the fall for killing that guy, he was clear that it wasn't him. Does Mom know more?"

Jack knew then that he'd never let them see the letter the DA had given back to him just that afternoon. It hadn't said just goodbye. It had said that Raymond hadn't planned to fall in love with Iris, to have six kids, but he'd made the mistake of becoming too comfortable in a life that he would never be allowed to have. He should have known he wouldn't be able to hide forever. Raymond O'Connell didn't exist, and he had to go, because the men that had shown up had made threats, and next time, it wouldn't be him they'd come for; it would be the kids, each of them. They wouldn't just disappear, either. Their bodies would be found one by one, and what would happen to them would be something from a parent's worst nightmare.

Even though Raymond had never said who he was, Jack knew that Iris not wanting her kids to see that letter had been the protective act of a mother. He knew Marcus would ask about it, and so would each of the siblings, so after Jack had pulled the letter from his jacket pocket that afternoon, he'd considered his actions for only a second before shredding it.

"You know what?" Jack lifted his tumbler and finished off the bourbon, feeling the bite. He stood up and took Karen's hand. "Let it go. Your mom's been through enough. Marcus, you have your job back, and disaster has been averted. We can question everything, but Raymond O'Connell wasn't who he said he was, and I, for one, can't imagine what it would've been like for your mom to learn this. He may have done the right thing and come back to clear her, but remember that all of this started because of him, so I'm going to say goodnight and take my wife home."

As he listened to the goodnights from everyone, seeing

the toll it had taken on them all, he took in the odd expression on Ryan's face.

"You said Raymond O'Connell was here?" Ryan said. "...Ray! This may sound totally crazy, but you know the boy who was over here, that friend of Alison's, Brady? She was just telling me this morning that they're leaving now, and they'd just moved here. She said that Brady's dad was named Ray, and he acted weird and said he knew me, and she thought he said he knew you too, Marcus. I don't know. Am I just looking for ghosts when there aren't any?"

Luke stared at Ryan, and the rest of them exchanged glances.

Owen stood up and said, "You know what, Ryan? Sounds like a reach. If it was good old Dad, then evidently, he's gone now, so at least he did the right thing. But remember, he left all of us a long time ago. So, that being said, I think Tessa and I are going to follow Jack and Karen and go home."

Then they all started to leave, to say goodnight, and no one said anything else about Raymond or the case.

As Jack started to his Mercedes and unlocked the door, Karen stopped him and ran her hands over his arms, his shoulders. He opened the door for her.

"You know I love you," she said. With Karen, he knew anything could be coming next.

"Okay," he said. "Yes, I love you too." He felt a smile tug at his lips as he waited for her to get in, skimming his hand over her butt and hip, letting it linger.

She lifted those mysterious O'Connell blue eyes, which were so vivid even in the dark of the Montana night. "You said this morning that you want to start a family, you know, have a baby…"

She suddenly seemed so shy as she lifted her hands over his shoulder and around his neck, settling against him, and there was a tightness in his chest, a hope that he didn't want her yanking away from him, so he said nothing at first, just stared long and hard at her.

"Come on," he finally prompted. "Don't leave me hanging."

"Well, I think you're right. I think now would be a great time to start a family."

He wasn't sure he'd heard her right. "You're serious?"

She slid her hand up the back of his neck, into his hair, and he lowered his face to hers, pressing his forehead to hers, pressing a kiss to her lips.

"Absolutely, one hundred percent," she said.

He shut his eyes for a second, feeling something he'd never expected. "Then let's get home before you change your mind," he said, and she laughed as she climbed into the car.

He watched Marcus, Charlotte, and Eva make their way across the street, and Owen and Tessa were already driving away. Harold and Suzanne, too, appeared to have figured things out.

He realized then that even though he was Jack Curtis, he was also one of the O'Connells.

Chapter Twenty

There was something about seeing him again. Her sons really had grown into his image, and she had to remind herself that he wasn't who she believed him to be.

He was older, but he still looked the same.

"Where have you been?" Iris said. There were so many things she could have asked, like how could he, and why, and who was he, really, considering Raymond O'Connell didn't exist? Those were the last words he'd ever said to her —that he didn't exist and that he was sorry.

Raymond just nodded, taking her in, before sitting down on one of the patio chairs out back. "You look good," he said.

So he wasn't really answering, just like in those last few months when he'd stopped going to work and strange men had started dropping by, and suddenly, the man she'd built a life with, whom she loved deeply, who was the father of her children, had become distant and pushed her away.

No, maybe, if she was honest with herself, she just hadn't seen the signs that had been there throughout their married life.

He glanced away. He seemed comfortable with the silence, and she realized Marcus did the same thing, and Ryan too, at times. Those eyes, the O'Connell blue, were his eyes, the eyes all her children had. Then there was the strength that had always oozed from him, even when he was walking away.

"Should I say the same about you?" she said. "Should we let this bullshit continue, with you not getting to the point and not answering my questions? I'm not the same woman you married. I had to figure out how to do it alone, but I did, Raymond—or whatever your name is. What should I call you?"

An odd smile touched the edges of his lips. "Just call me Ray. I see you still have that fight in you. It's what drew me to you, Iris. I've never met anyone like you since."

She wasn't sure how to take that, so she said nothing, wondering why he'd suddenly just shown up here, and why now.

"Why didn't you tell anyone what happened?" he said, questioning her with his eyes. "After all these years, Iris, you said nothing."

She considered what to say. "You know, having a daughter who's a lawyer, I've listened to everything she said, everything about how spouses can't be compelled to share secrets about one another. It did give me some peace to know that the more I said nothing, I wasn't just digging myself into a grave. I wondered something else, though, too, and I never got an answer from Karen, because how do you ask your own daughter how the law applies when you don't believe your marriage is real? I mean, you picked a name, Raymond O'Connell. Isn't that what you said? It was the name I took, the name on the birth certificates of our children, but it's not who you really are. Isn't that what you said before you left, when you told me what would've happened to my children?"

He only nodded and looked away. "Why did you keep the letter?"

She had to pull her gaze from him, joining him on the other patio chair in the backyard. Luke was still over at Ryan's, and she was glad for that, as she just couldn't make herself be around her children. She needed a moment to breathe, to shake off the shame she knew she shouldn't carry, the shame of being fingerprinted and photographed like a common criminal and staring at bars in a crowded cell all night, wondering if that would be her life.

"I don't know," she said. "Guess I couldn't make myself throw it out, after what happened. I needed to read the words, the warning, the explanation of why you'd left. I needed to be told that the fairytale I thought I was living was a fantasy. Maybe it was the only sane thing I could hold on to after putting a knife into a man. I did it because I knew it was what they had planned for you. You know I still see his eyes, the way he looked at me, reached out to me, grabbed me as he went down? I heard the life leave his body. I mean, how does anyone ever come to terms with killing someone? How can you sleep peacefully at night, knowing you stole someone's life?"

He moved the chair closer and leaned forward, resting his forearms on his knees. She could feel him. She wished he wouldn't, because he'd stolen her dream from her, their life, and the man she'd wanted him to be.

"You want to hear that it gets easier?" He shook his head, then pulled in a breath. "The first one stays with you. But I never understood why you killed him."

She remembered what the men had called him: David. So that was his name. He didn't look like a David.

"Really? He threatened you. I heard what he said, that

your time was up. There was just something about him. I had a feeling I'd never had about someone before, as if he were pure evil, as if he would've killed you without a thought—and the kids upstairs, too. But I didn't know it until I read it in the letter you left. I was acting on a mother's instinct only. All I could think was that you'd done something, that I didn't know you, that they'd found you and were going to take you back to answer for whatever you'd done. Remember what he said, that one night the kids would go to sleep and not wake up? I had no choice. It was fear that drove me. Strangers had shown up and were destroying my family. Did I have a choice?"

She just shook her head. "I guess I never really understood which government they were from. Israel, is that what you said? You were, what, a spy who had somehow found himself working as a mechanic in small-town America? A big chunk of what happened that night was gone when I woke up on the floor. The knife was in my hand, and there was just blood, and the man I had stabbed was gone, and the other one, too. My head hurt so bad, and for a moment I had no idea what happened. It's a black hole, but you were there. I remember your face, looking at me. It was like a dream. That was all I could think…" She gestured toward him.

She wasn't sure why, but she expected him to say something that would explain that night, the night that had begun the rest of her life, taking away her dream of growing old with him. Why, as he sat there now, couldn't she find it in herself to hate him?

"Too many secrets, I see," she finally said. "You know that Owen came downstairs. It was the creak of the stairs and his voice, I think, that woke me on the floor. I don't know what happened, but all of a sudden, I heard his footsteps. The knife was still there, so I grabbed your handkerchief and wrapped it up. Seeing so much blood, I wasn't thinking straight. When I turned, he was right there, staring at your office, which was a disaster. That man was going to kill you, and then what would he have done to our children? His blood was on the floor, and I didn't think. I just knew I had to get Owen out of there.

"I will never forget the look on his face. I gave Owen the knife, wrapped up, and told him to get rid of it. I expected him to throw it in the garbage, but he buried it in the woods. I never asked him what he'd done with it. I just assumed. Can you believe I did that? What kind of mother does that to her teenage son? I said I needed his help to keep us together, and I sat the kids down the next morning and told them you were gone and never coming back. It was just us. I don't know how I found the words. I robbed Owen of his carefree teenage years. That's all I've been able to think ever since I learned about what he did. Instead of hiding everything, I created a problem for all my children."

She lifted her hands, because with everything that had happened that night, which was now a big black hole, she had more questions than answers. Now, the man responsible was sitting right there, and she knew she couldn't tell anyone.

Raymond was leaning forward, his hands clasped, and she knew there was anger simmering there. For her? Maybe. He said nothing. So many damn secrets.

"What happened that I ended up on the floor?" she said. "I just remember waking up."

He lifted his gaze, and she took in the hardness that filled his expression. "You were knocked out. I thought the other guy had killed you, and maybe he planned to, but I grabbed our tarp—remember, the new one I'd just bought to cover the wood out back for the fireplace I was planning on putting in?"

She hadn't thought of that in years.

"We moved the body out, buried it at the edge of Lionel Shepard's property in the park. Driving in there was easy because Lionel was drinking again, even though no one knew. The DNA wasn't in the system, and the body couldn't be identified if the teeth weren't there, so I made sure of that. I couldn't have anything bringing attention here, to you, to the kids. My time was up. When I made it home and found you still on the floor, I was furious the other guy had hit you so hard, but you were breathing. I wrote you that letter and tried to explain what I could. I packed nothing. I waited until I heard you stirring and knew you would wake up, and I heard one of the kids on the stairs. I never meant to leave the blood for you to clean up, but I don't understand why you kept the letter. You touched it with your bloody hands, the blood that matched that body buried out there. When I saw the news, it didn't take long for me to put the pieces together."

"And yet here you are, back here in Livingston. Where have you been? I already asked you. Did you come back just for me, for this mess, to clear it up?" she said. Again he glanced away, and she really looked at him. "Ray, or whatever your name is, I think I have a right to know where you went, why you're here now, and who you really are, don't you think?"

"Raymond O'Connell didn't exist before 1983. Then he suddenly did. He met a woman, a smart, gorgeous, feisty woman who'd make the perfect cover. I never expected to fall head over heels in love with you. I worked for Mossad. You know countries have their own people, spies planted everywhere, in every society, to keep an eye on what other governments are doing. I was to fit in, having the perfect, normal all-American family. I had a great cover working as a mechanic, taking nonexistent contracts for the railroad. You didn't know that, did you?"

The way he said it, the hurt she'd thought had long since disappeared came back, but thankfully not with the same intensity.

"Those overnight shifts I had to work, being away from home for days at a time, on the railroad…"

"You were a spy for another country," she said. "I was your cover. So what does that make our children?"

He said nothing for a second. "You did an amazing job, alone. Walking away was the hardest thing I ever did, but the choice to stay would've put a target on you. I was called home. I had made a mistake, and it would've cost me my cover…"

For a moment, she wasn't sure what he was saying. Then she knew.

"You cheated on me," she said.

He shut his eyes for a second and glanced away. This was the one thing she'd never expected, and she felt enormous rage sweep over her, through her. She stood up and slapped him across the face, and the sound echoed in the quiet night.

He stood, too, right in front of her, so damn close. She'd forgotten how tall he was, standing before him. She hated the fact that she still loved him. She went to slap him again, but he grabbed her wrist so fast and held it.

"My son's name is Brady," he said. "We moved here a few months ago. I knew I was playing with fire when he met your granddaughter—my granddaughter, Alison. She was with Eva, little Eva, the girl Marcus adopted. I knew then that it was only a matter of time before we'd have to leave."

She pulled her hand away, realizing what he was

saying. "The nice boy that Alison is infatuated with romantically is your son?" It was horrifying, and she knew the knowledge would gut Alison after everything she'd been through.

He didn't nod. "We'll be leaving in the morning."

"You said you're here with your son, not his mother?" She didn't know why she was punishing herself by asking, but maybe she didn't want any more of the lies she'd lived with. Whoever had said that the truth would set you free had no idea of the pain it could bring.

"No, just the two of us," he said. "Brady's mother died when he was young."

She nodded. "Should I ask how she died?" she said. Did she really want to know? She wanted to step back as she took in his odd smile. He looked down on her with the same charisma he'd had so long ago, and it had her wanting to do anything for him, but she wasn't that same stupid young woman who believed in happily ever after.

"Nothing like what you're imagining," he said. "It was a car accident when Brady was two."

She only nodded, wondering if he had loved her, as well. That, she didn't want to know.

"So, Ray, are you still a hunted man? Is there still a target on my children?"

He glanced away. "You know Luke has been looking for me for a long time. I was kind of amused at first when I learned who he'd become, working in the special forces, doing things for his country that he's not allowed to talk about. I learned that Marcus was the local sheriff, and Ryan was the law of the parks. Kind of fitting, I thought. I learned that Suzanne, sweet little Suzanne, the colicky one, had gotten screwed over by the fire department, who'd never have accepted her anyway. Owen is a plumber, and he seems to finally be happy. And then there was Karen.

Even though I loved all my kids, and a parent is never supposed to admit to having a favorite, Karen was mine, because she was a mini you in every way. The fight, the passion, the personality. She was the spitting image of you, the older she got. The worst day of my life was the November day that I walked away—and I had to walk away. But I found a way to keep an eye out from a distance. As the years passed, I expected you to find someone else, but you never did."

He lifted his hand to touch her cheek, and she should have pulled back, but then he did so before he could touch her. He dropped his hand.

She heard a vehicle and knew it was Luke in his old pickup. She could see the headlights from the side of the house. "Luke's home," she said.

Raymond nodded, stepped back, and then reached over and ran his hand over her arm before pulling away. "Goodbye, Iris," was all he said, and then the man she loved was gone, walking away into the darkness.

Just then, the sliding glass door opened from the house, and Luke stepped out and said, "There you are."

She forced a smile to her face even though that one touch from Raymond had completely unsettled her. "Just getting some air and thinking," she replied.

"Well, everyone missed you tonight. Was thinking, if you're okay with it, about having a barbecue here tomorrow, and…"

Luke had walked back into the house, and she had stopped listening. She knew he was trying to bring some sense of normalcy back into her life, but she couldn't help herself as she hesitated in the doorway and glanced out into the darkness, toward the back gate, where Raymond had come from. She wondered if she'd ever see him again.

Then she made herself pull in a breath and step into

the house, hearing Luke still talking about plans and family. She took a second to remind herself that despite the hatred she had for Raymond over what he'd done, she also should've thanked him for the six amazing children who had made her into the person she was today. They had filled her with a love she wouldn't have traded and a life she wouldn't give up.

"You know what, Luke?" she said. "Yeah, a family barbecue tomorrow would be perfect."

Turn the page for a sneak peek of
THE FALLEN O'CONNELL
Available in print, eBook & coming soon to audio

The Fallen O'Connell

THE O'CONNELLS

Thirty-five years ago, Raymond O'Connell didn't exist, at least not until the moment Iris walked into his life. His very existence had been a secret, a carefully cultivated lie, except for the fact that he loved Iris and the six children he'd never planned on having. He'd become careless, living a life that belonged to someone else.

Becoming Raymond O'Connell had made him forget who he really was, and when he fell in love with a fantasy he knew he couldn't have, he put his family in danger. Ultimately, he found himself covering up a murder to protect the woman he loved, and that act forced him to walk away and return to the shadows of a secret life that he couldn't find his way out of.

When he returns to Livingston with a son in tow, what he doesn't expect is to be dragged from the shadows to protect a family that suddenly has a target on their backs. Soon, Raymond finds himself becoming part of a bigger, deadlier plot—one that could leave someone in his family, someone he's sworn to stay away from, dead.

The choice he'll have to make to protect the O'Connells could come at a heartbreaking cost. Can Raymond choose between the son he has now and the family he walked away from?

The Fallen O'Connell, Chapter 1

R aymond stared at the old shag carpet, listening to the thump of footsteps and then the water running upstairs. How had his son suddenly found his voice of damned independence for the first time in his life?

Brady was refusing to leave a home that was never supposed to have been permanent. Where had this stubborn streak come from, this sudden determination that he wouldn't have his life upended anymore? Yes, those had been his exact words, and now Raymond was at a loss for how to get his teenage son out the door and onto a plane. This was a dilemma he'd never thought he'd have.

Raymond had lived and breathed looking over his shoulder, but he couldn't explain why he found himself staring at the locked front door now, knowing the deadbolt would keep out no one who really wanted to get into the dated old house. Worse yet was the secret that lay behind why they couldn't stay in Livingston, why they had come and were now leaving. The reason, which he never planned to share with his son, was that he'd had to see in person the family he'd deserted.

Now here he was, waiting in his kitchen, knowing he was going to have to sit his son down for a talk he didn't want to have. He listened to the footsteps upstairs and glanced at his watch. It was early for Brady to be up on a Saturday morning, even though it was close to noon.

When he heard him on the stairs, his phone dinged with another email message: an inquiry from the Barbados cottage he'd booked and paid for, the one they were supposed to have arrived at the week before.

Brady gave him only a passing glance as he stepped off the last stair, barefoot, his dark hair sticking up. His eyes were his mother's, but his face and the way he walked… Raymond realized his son looked like Marcus, or maybe Luke.

He was staring at Brady's back as he reached into the fridge for a jug of milk and then into the cupboard for a bowl, and he could see how deeply ready his son was, by the expression on his face, to go another round with him. Brady set the bowl down, reached for a box of corn flakes, and dumped in the cereal, then milk. Because Raymond was standing in front of the drawer that held the spoons, he wondered whether his son would keep up the silent treatment or ask him to move.

There was the standoff.

Raymond pulled in a breath and tossed a large spoon on the counter. "Saves you having to ask, since I can see you're still doing your best to give me the silent treatment."

His son didn't flinch but snatched the spoon, then walked down over to the old table and pulled out a chair, still barefoot, in a pair of sweats and an old T-shirt.

"So, about Barbados," Raymond said, "I think we need to have another conversation, because we can't stay here."

"I'm not leaving," Brady said. "I told you that, so don't

think you can strongarm me, because you can't. I told you already that I like it here. You're the vagabond who has never been able to stay in one spot long, needing to see the world, but not me. I want roots and friends, and I'm finishing school here." He shoved another spoonful of cereal in his mouth and didn't look over to him.

Raymond had to fight the urge to yell, to demand that he get his ass upstairs and pack, because he was his father and he decided when they left and when they stayed. But he'd already done that, and it had backfired. Hence, they were still there.

What had his son said but "You can't make me"? And so far, he'd been right. Maybe he needed to try the reasoning approach.

"Okay, I see you're still angry…"

"You're kidding, right?" Brady tossed down his spoon and looked up to him. "You texted Alison that we were leaving, on my phone, as if it was from me. She's my friend! I like her, and you had no right. You crossed so many lines, Dad."

Okay, maybe he had crossed a line, but his son had never pulled something like this before, basically refusing to listen to him. Worse, Brady had no idea the danger he was putting them in.

"Fine, I get it," Raymond said. "You made your point, but you don't understand. We have to leave. This was a mistake, coming here—"

"You keep saying that." Brady cut him off, not something he had done until now. "But when I ask you why, you treat me like I'm just a little kid who's supposed to listen and fall in line without questioning anything you decide. You say it's not my concern or that, my all-time favorite, you're my father and you know best. Well, I hate to tell you this, Dad, but you don't know what's best for me. If you did, you wouldn't be trying to rip me away yet again from a place I like and a girl I'm partial to. You seem to forget I'm eighteen…"

"Not yet, you're not."

Brady slapped both his hands to the tabletop, the sound ricocheting through the half-empty house. "In three weeks I will be. I'm not a kid anymore who's going to be shuffled from one city or country to another, to places where I can't put pictures up or have a room that's always mine. Then there's Alison, who I like a lot."

All Raymond could do was stand in horror, wondering how this had spun so far out of control—out of his control. "Alison is nothing but trouble, Brady. I told you that, and her family is going through some tough times. She's not someone you can be involved with."

Brady inclined his head as if working out a kink. Raymond had never seen this kind of passion and readiness to fight in him. "I hear you, Dad, but I like Alison, and last I looked, this is a democracy, not a dictatorship. You don't get to pick my friends or who I hang out with or who my girlfriend is. And Alison isn't trouble. She makes me laugh and smile. So no, I'm not leaving." Brady picked up his spoon again and dug into his cereal.

Raymond picked up his phone, tapping the screen. "Barbados is a great place. We'd have a cottage on the white sandy beach. We've talked about going for a long time. Look, it was supposed to be a surprise, and maybe I didn't handle this right. I shouldn't have texted Alison for you. I hear you, and I'm sorry, if that will help. I promise you, this time we'll stay put for longer. You can make some friends, take up diving like we talked about."

He walked over to his son, who was working a giant mouthful of milk and cereal, and held out his cell phone to show him the image of the cottage and baby-blue ocean, but Brady only looked up to him after glancing briefly at the image as if it meant nothing.

"Not right now," he said. "I told you that. It looks nice, Dad, but I'm not going. I'm not leaving Alison right now. I've been dragged everywhere for years, but no more. I'm finishing school here. I have friends and Alison. I need to get ready." He shoved in his last mouthful of cereal before grabbing his bowl and taking it to the sink to rinse it out.

"Get ready for what?" Raymond said. They had to leave Livingston, yet his kid was far too determined, far too independent for his liking. Even though he had known this day was coming, this was a side of his son he'd never expected to see.

"I have a date for a wedding," Brady said.

"A wedding, what wedding? Who's getting married?"

Brady left the bowl in the sink and started to leave the kitchen, but he stopped in the archway and looked back at his dad before shrugging. "Alison's parents are, and I'm her date. I need to hurry, because I promised her I'd be there at one, and I still need to shower and dress."

Then his son was gone, and all Raymond could do was think of what a problem this was. His son was too stubborn, and another of his sons was getting married.

He knew there was no way this Alison and Brady thing could continue, but he also knew that leaving town without Brady ever learning the truth was now completely off the table. He couldn't stop his son from walking out the door right now and going to this wedding.

"Shit," he said. This was just another thing he'd somehow lost control of.

About the Author

"Lorhainne Eckhart is one of my go to authors when I want a guaranteed good book. So many twists and turns, but also so much love and such a strong sense of family."

(Lora W., Reviewer)

New York Times & USA Today bestseller Lorhainne Eckhart writes Raw Relatable Real Romance is best known for her big family romances series, where "Morals and family are running themes. Danger, romance, and a drive to do what is right will see you glued to the page." As one fan calls her, she is the "Queen of the family saga." (aherman) writing "the ups and downs of what goes on within a family but also with some suspense, angst and of course a bit of romance thrown in for good measure." Follow Lorhainne on Bookbub to receive alerts on New Releases and Sales and join her mailing list at LorhainneEckhart.com for her Monday Blog, books news, giveaways and FREE reads. With over 120 books, audiobooks, and multiple series published and available at all retailers now translated into six languages. She is a multiple recipient of the Readers' Favorite Award for Suspense and Romance, and lives in the Pacific Northwest on an island, is the mother of three, her oldest has autism and she is an advocate for never giving up on your dreams.

"Lorhainne Eckhart has this uncanny way of just hitting the spot every time with her books."

(Caroline L., Reviewer)

The O'Connells: *The O'Connells of Livingston, Montana are not your typical family. A riveting collection of stories surrounding the ups and downs of what goes on within a family but also with some suspense, angst and of course a bit of romance thrown in for good measure "I thought I loved the Friessens, but I absolutely adore the O'Connell's. Each and every book has totally different genres of stories but the one thing in common is how she is able to wrap it around the family which is the heart of each story." (C. Logue)*

The Friessens: *An emotional big family romance series, the Friessen family siblings find their relationships tested, lay their hearts on the line, and discover lasting love! "Lorhainne Eckhart is one of my go to authors when I want a guaranteed good book. So many twists and turns, but also so much love and such a strong sense of family." (Lora W., Reviewer)*

The Parker Sisters: *The Parker Sisters are a close-knit family, and like any other family they have their ups and downs. "Eckhart has crafted another intense family drama… The character development is outstanding, and the emotional investment is high…" (Aherman, Reviewer)*

***The McCabe Brothers:** Join the five McCabe siblings on their journeys to the dark and dangerous side of love! An intense, exhilarating collection of romantic thrillers you won't want to miss. — "Eckhart has a new series that is definitely worth the read. The queen of the family saga started this series with a spin-off of her wildly successful Friessen series." From a Readers' Favorite award—winning author and "queen of the family saga" (Aherman)*

Lorhainne loves to hear from her readers! You can connect with me at:
www.LorhainneEckhart.com
lorhainneeckhart.le@gmail.com

In the Family
In the Silence
In the Charm
Unexpected Consequences
It Was Always You
The First Time I Saw You
Welcome to My Arms
Welcome to Boston
I'll Always Love You
Ground Rules
A Reason to Breathe
You Are My Everything
Anything For You
The Homecoming
Stay Away From My Daughter
The Bad Boy
A Place of Our Own
The Visitor
All About Devon
Long Past Dawn
How to Heal a Heart
Keep Me in Your Heart

The O'Connells
The Neighbor
The Third Call
The Secret Husband
The Quiet Day
The Commitment
The Missing Father
The Hometown Hero
Justice
The Family Secret
The Fallen O'Connell

The Return of the O'Connells
And The She Was Gone
The Stalker
The O'Connell Family Christmas
The Girl Next Door
Broken Promises

The McCabe Brothers
Don't Stop Me (Vic)
Don't Catch Me (Chase)
Don't Run From Me (Aaron)
Don't Hide From Me (Luc)
Don't Leave Me (Claudia)
Out of Time

A Billy Jo McCabe Mystery
Nothing As it Seems
Hiding in Plain Sight
The Cold Case
The Trap
Above the Law

The Wilde Brothers
The One (Joe and Margaret)
The Honeymoon, A Wilde Brothers Short
Friendly Fire (Logan and Julia)
Not Quite Married, A Wilde Brothers Short
A Matter of Trust (Ben and Carrie)
The Reckoning, A Wilde Brothers Christmas
Traded (Jake)
Unforgiven (Samuel)
The Holiday Bride

Married in Montana

His Promise
Love's Promise
A Promise of Forever

The Parker Sisters
Thrill of the Chase
The Dating Game
Play Hard to Get
What We Can't Have
Go Your Own Way
A June Wedding

Kate & Walker
One Night
Edge of Night
Last Night

Walk the Right Road Series
The Choice
Lost and Found
Merkaba
Bounty
Blown Away: The Final Chapter

The Saved Series
Saved
Vanished
Captured

Single Titles
He Came Back
Loving Christine

For my German Readers

Die Außenseiter-Reihe
Der Vergessene Junge
Der Gefallene Held

For my French Readers
L'ENFANT OUBLIÉ